INNOCENT DECEPTION

BONNIE MINOR

authorHOUSE®

AuthorHouse™
1663 Liberty Drive
Bloomington, IN 47403
www.authorhouse.com
Phone: 1 (800) 839-8640

Published by AuthorHouse 01/16/2016

ISBN: 978-1-5049-7299-4 (sc)
ISBN: 978-1-5049-7300-7 (e)

Print information available on the last page.

Author: Bonnie Minor

This is my first novel. My mother encouraged me to write it. I had a dream, woke up and started writing it took me 3 days to write it down. I couldn't stop, from laughter to tears.

Funny Innocence of Youth:

Shar McCoy couldn't wait to get off the ranch and go into the Big City to make a name for herself as a fashion designer. When her naive ways and passionate eyes get her into trouble with love. Love bound them together, fate pulled them apart. Maybe the ranch wasn't such a bad place to live after all.

TABLE OF CONTENTS

CHAPTER 1

Everyone moved forward in the terminal line except Shar McCoy. She felt a numb drawing sensation in the pit of her stomach as she stood there waiting for her plane to come in. Her mind was going back over the past few months. Why couldn't John understand her need to go to school to be something in life other than just being happy to marry him and wait for him to come back from the service, to continue their life as man and wife? Why did I have to pick a fight before he left? "Why couldn't you just be happy; like me; to get married and wait patiently for him to return?" Lucy, my best friend, had said; not understanding me for the first time in our lives. We had grown up together, always doing everything, sharing everything, even dating together. It sounded good, when in our senior year, we both got engaged and decided to have a double wedding. But, as summer drew nearer, I knew that there was more to life I hadn't experienced yet; that part of me could not give up my freedom. The freedom I hadn't even tasted yet. For growing up in a small town and having very strict parents, I had never really been on my own yet. Of course, I loved John in my own way; if he could only wait for a few years. But, the way he went off in such a huff when we broke up, I'll probably never see him again.

Shar's thoughts were interrupted when Jeff; the airport attendant in Yakima; said "Hey Shar; If you are catching this plane out you had better get your luggage checked in. Of course wouldn't mind ya staying round here, for there ain't a girl in a hundred miles looks half as pretty as you." Oh! be quiet before my head pops. But thanks for the compliment; I needed a boost." "Well, maybe you'll be rich and famous someday and remember this country boy." He laughed. Jeff always had a good sense of humor, even though he was too tall and awkward to be cute.

She boarded the small plane and took a seat over the wing so she could look out over the valley as she left. There was a sad feeling to be leaving the valley she had grown up in. It was going to be a big change for her to go to a big city. She would have to try and remember what her mom had said. Yes, it would be hard for her not to trust everyone she met and not to smile at everyone as if they were old friends. That is just the way it is in a small farm community; you even make strangers feel welcome. But mom had said you can't do that in the city. It must be a strange way of life, having to hide your feelings, but I can do it if that's what it takes.

She had decided to go to Denver to become a fashion designer. She was pretty enough to be a model with her golden blonde hair hanging silkily down to the middle of her shoulders; Icey blue eyes under dark lashes and eyebrows, set above high distinct cheekbones with her tilted nose and square jaw that gave her a certain determined look; which let everyone know that she usually got her own way in the end. She walked of the plane with a certain air of poise. Even though she wore tight blue jeans and a lose sweat shirt; you would think by the way she looked in them that they had been designed for her.

As she boarded the next plane in Portland it was starting to rain. This was going to be a long day before it was over she thought as she picked up a magazine that was in the seat by hers on the plane. Psychology Today didn't they have anything better than that to read? Well, maybe I can just stare down at the top of the clouds all the way to Denver. "Excuse me, but you're holding my magazine. If you don't intend to read it, may I finish the article I was on?" Shar turned to stare into a pair of the smokiest grey eyes she had ever seen. A fleeting feeling of excitement surged through her veins.

Looking at his blonde hair and mustache, and his flashy white teeth; he looked like something you would pull out of a TV commercial. Her flesh turned pink as she realized she must be staring. "Oh!" She stammered, and handed him his book. "That must have been a juicy article from the looks of your face." "I-I wasn't reading." He raised his brows; "Well then does that mean those looks were for me?" he laughed. "No I was thinking of-of someone else." "Who is the lucky fellow?" he sneered. "It's none of your business!" she replied. "You were so eager to get your article back; why don't you read it and stop trying to play psychologist with me?" "Well, I would not mind playing doctor with you, but not here please; this plane is crowded you know; it might cramp my style." He laughed. An infuriatingly teasing laugh showing her how much he was enjoying the embarrassing spot she had gotten herself into. She knew she hated him for his self-assurance and arrogance. This was going to be one flight that she couldn't wait to end.

Looking down at her lap she realized how light her golden skin was against his dark bronze tan, as his arm was on the arm rest now; no more than an inch from hers. He was wearing a polo shirt and casual dress slacks; but every inch of him screamed class. I wonder what he does for a living? She thought. He is probably a psychologist or teacher reading that garbage. I wonder if he is married. (She tried to forget he was there) but try as she would she could not keep her mind off of him. It made her blood tingle just to imagine what it would be like to be in his arms. What craziness! John hadn't even affected her like this; and with him it was real. She tried harder to put him out of her thoughts by thinking of the ad she had answered to the Flair Clothing Department Company in Denver; that would enable her to work and go to school at the same time. Even though she didn't really need the money, the experience would be good and she didn't like the idea of always counting on Dad to give her everything she wanted. She was pampered as most rich girls are; but growing up on the ranch her Dad had had taught her to be self- sufficient (He lived by the motto "If it's worth having, it's worth working for). Sometimes, when things got hectic and a couple of their combine drivers wouldn't show up to work she would help her Dad and drive one all day. Or if a truck driver didn't show up she would take over there. When the wheat was ripe it didn't wait for anyone.

The man next to her said, "I hate to interrupt your train of thought little miss, but you'd better buckle up. We're going to be hitting some turbulence up ahead. You were too tuned out to hear the stewardess." "I'm sorry. I must have dozed off there." she said blinking her eyes sleepily and giving him her down home smile, before she caught herself and realized the impression she must be giving. Oh, if she could just turn back the clock and start over. This is one person she would like to start over with! Then she remembered how arrogant he had been and decided why waste the effort.

The airplane jerked then and she grabbed a hold of the arms of her seat; her fingers turning white. He reached out and put a hand on hers. "Just relax, we'll be through it in a minute." He grinned reassuringly. She started to relax a little, but the sensation his hand on hers was sending her brain told her she had a lot more to fear than just the plane. She had never lost control of her thoughts the way she had been today. Maybe it's just everything that's been happening to me so fast she rationalized. Looking at him she said "I'm alright now." He never moved his hand. She had to get that hand off of hers. She felt like her hand was going to melt, and with it she would lose her own identity. She looked into his eyes to confirm the fact that she was OK, but as their eyes met she felt a passion awaken in her that she never knew existed. She yanked her hand from his. His eyes turned hard and cold so fast that it frightened her. She turned and stared out the window again. What was it with this stranger that made her act so dumb? "Sorry if I offended you." he said coldly. "I was trying to be reassuring. I didn't realize you would think I was a mad rapist. Of course I didn't take into consideration that you're still wet behind the ears." She was boiling now. What gave him the right to start judging her? "Well maybe I am." she exclaimed, "But I would rather be anything than a pompous, stuck on himself, snob like you are."

The plane was starting to descend and the stewardess was saying what a pleasure flying had been. Everyone was unbuckling their seat belts and not a minute too soon. She knew if she had to sit by him another minute she would break down and cry. She couldn't do that. Not after what he had said about her still being wet behind the ears.

Mark was smiling down at her. "Ladies before gentlemen. I don't want it to get around that I am not a gentleman; even if you don't act much like a lady." Shar got to her feet, so mad, that she couldn't even think of anything to say; so she just walked briskly on out of the plane and down the steps toward the terminal. She just knew that she had to get away from this man, who for some strange reason had had such an overpowering effect on her; and who apparently could care less if she even existed.

Shar couldn't help over hearing the well-dressed woman who ran up and threw her arms around his neck. "Oh, Mark darling I'm sorry I was late; but you know how the traffic can be, and try as he would the chauffer just couldn't get through any faster." Standing clutching Mark's arm at the baggage claim, looking longingly up at him the woman said, "Mark darling I have missed you so much I just don't know what I would have done with myself if you would have stayed away another minute. I was so bored without you." Shar found her luggage and lifted it off. She looked around wondering if maybe the traffic was really that bad. She hadn't decided whether to rent a car or just take a cab. Well, there would be time to worry about that tomorrow. She should try to get a cab to take her stuff to the Hilton, as she had a room reserved there for a week to give her time to find herself a place and get settled in. As she looked out of the terminal a man standing next to a cab asked if he could be of service. "Yes. Maybe. I need a ride to the Hilton. I have a room reserved there." "Well, the van that goes there is parked just five cars back, but if you like I'll give you a lift." "Yes. That would be nice. I don't really feel like being sociable with a lot of other guests right now. All I want is a shower and a bed." She climbed in and he put her things in the trunk and off they went.

The city lights were unbelievable and so were the mountains coming in on the plane. I wonder what it looks like in the daylight she thought. Tomorrow I will go out and explore, but tonight just let me rest and collect myself. This day had sure done her nerves in.

The car pulled up to the lobby and he was now helping a doorman get her luggage out. The doorman followed her up to the desk where she got her key and room number. She was on the 6th floor. Well, at least they had an elevator and she should have a good view from that high up. In Yakima the highest building was 3 stories, and only a couple of them. She thought how different this was and excitement welled up in her as she entered the elevator and told the doorman which floor. She tipped the doorman when he brought her luggage in. She walked to the windows and drew open the curtains. To her surprise, there was a balcony, so she stepped out on it for a better look. It was overwhelming! The city lights were of such magnitude that she felt like it was Christmas and she was a little girl again. Down below you could see the greenery of the garden lit up with special lighting effects, and the pool with a slight steam rising from it as it was a little cool this time of the evening. Guess I'd better go take a bath and get a bite to eat if I'm going to get any sleep tonight. I must start looking for a place tomorrow. She turned, restless now, and walked back into the lonely room.

Her mind went back over the afternoon and she remembered the woman calling him Mark darling. Well, at least now her fantasy could have a name she thought as she picked her clothes out and hung them up. She decided to wear a light sun dress with dark blue miniature flowers, down to the lounge for a bite to eat. She pulled a shawl over her shoulders just in case it might be a little chilly. The band was starting to play as she sat down. She felt a little homesick as she picked up the menu. She decided on a chef salad and a glass of milk. As the waitress left she realized that this was going to be her new life style! She might as well try to enjoy eating alone. It sure was a lot different than the meals back home where Mom and Dad had always discussed the events of the day and what was on the agenda for tomorrow. Funny; that back then I never realized how happy meals could be or even thought about how it would be by myself.

CHAPTER 2

A man had stopped by her table. She looked up. "Did you want something?" she asked. "Well maybe." He said, with a half awkward grin. "I just couldn't help noticing the look on your face. It looked as though you had lost your last friend. I know I hate to eat alone, so I thought maybe we could keep each other company through dinner. I promise I'll mind my manners." Holding up his hand like a boy scout he said, "Scouts honor." With his dark curly hair and dancing eyes; Shar laughed at his impression of a boy scout. She smiled and said "Sure! No sense in both of us being miserable through dinner." "Now that's what I like." he said. "A sensible girl. They're a rare breed these days." As he pulled the chair back and sat down Shar blushed remembering her mother's warning. "My name is Tom Henley; what's yours?" For a second Shar hesitated; then thought what harm could exchanging names do? He had already told her his. "Shar McCoy," she stated, trying to sound formal, in case he found her overly friendly. Her salad arrived then. He told the waitress to have his meal brought over to her table and told her where he had been sitting. It was a couple of minutes until his dinner arrived. He thanked her and turned his attention back to Shar. "As I was saying, I'm up here for a lawyer's convention, and I really don't know anyone here yet other than a few corporate lawyers I met today; but they live here so they aren't staying at the hotel. You haven't said two words all the time I've been sitting here." he commented. "You seem to be a million miles away." Shar didn't know why she was comparing him to Mark. Tom was very attractive; with his firm straight mouth and dimples. His perfect grey suit and black lashes that outlined his dancing eyes gave you the impression that you were the only ornate object in the world. Why didn't she feel like she had with Mark? Why wasn't this man who apparently charmed his way through life, and probably had the girls eating out of his hands, making her even the least bit nervous? She couldn't understand. Maybe it was just the flight, she told herself.

"Well, I'm here to live. I have a job here and plan to start college here this fall." Before she knew it, she was telling him everything about her past and how it had brought her to this point in her life. But, she left out the part about her flight in to Denver. They had both finished eating and Shar decided that it was getting pretty late so she tried to excuse herself to go upstairs. He caught her arm and said "One dance, then I'll let you go. Remember your country manners. You can't just eat and run." With his gentle attitude, she couldn't just walk off. "OK. One." she said, holding up one finger. "Then it's off to bed for me." "Don't be too inviting" he commented laughingly. "If I wasn't a gentleman I might try to take advantage of your naivetés." Smiling down at her he kissed her lightly on the forehead. She might have been frightened if it hadn't reminded her of the way her Dad had always kissed her goodnight. He pulled her a little closer as the music picked up a little and he started to whirl her around the floor. She was thankful for the ballroom dancing her parents had made her take, for he was an expert and she didn't shame him.

The dance ended as abruptly as it had started, and Tom said he would see her to her room. She protested, but Tom said "It's not safe to let a young beautiful girl such as yourself go wandering around the halls this time of night." As they entered the 6th floor there were a couple of middle aged, intoxicated gentlemen and she was glad Tom was there. That was when she realized how vulnerable she really was here in this big city. When I find a place I'll need roommates she thought. They were at her door and she was afraid to unlock it because she had really just met Tom. What did she really know about him? She turned and said "Goodnight Tom, it was nice meeting you." He winked and said "Likewise; can I see you tomorrow Shar?" Before she even thought she said, "Breakfast at 8 don't be late!" He smiled. "Wear something you can walk in and I'll show you the city. I have a car and it sure beats walking everywhere or paying a cab to drive you." He laughed and walked down the hall toward the elevator. He turned saying, "You'd better go in before I change my mind and come back." He waved as he stepped into the elevator and she closed the door behind her.

As she slipped into her night gown and crawled into the crispy fresh sheets, her mind went back over the events of the day. When her head hit the pillow though she was fast asleep. Morning came awfully early she thought as she opened her eyes and stared around in a daze. Where am I she thought for a moment, then she remembered? She looked at the clock. It was 7 o'clock. How could I sleep so late she wondered, then realizing that with the curtains shut and no sound of birds to wake her she had slept in. She ran into the shower. She would be lucky now if she could get ready to meet Tom for breakfast, and she remembered her saying don't be late. She didn't realize how much she was looking forward to spending the day with him until now. She dried off, noticing her well-built shape that she had acquired over the years through diet and plenty of exercise. She picked her clothes out with careful consideration and decided to wear the red pin striped pedal pusher with jacket that matched, a white silky blouse, and white tennis shoes. After all, he did say wear something you can walk in. She pulled one side of her hair up in a comb and put a final touch of lipstick on her lips. Then as a last minute thought, she grabbed a red scarf and tied it around her neck. Perfect, she thought grabbing her purse and headed for the door. Just as she opened it, his hand stopped in mid-air. "Sensational!" He said, looking her over from head to toe. His eyes seemed to be taking off all of the clothes she had just worked so hard to put on. Catching her hand, he said, "Come on our table is waiting."

They walked down to the elevator. Tom looked very masculine in his snug fitting white jeans and light blue sport shirt with a white wind breaker. He was a perfect escort. A girl would have to be crazy not to like him. They entered the lobby, but instead of turning into the lounge, he caught her arm and said "Hope you don't mind, but I reserved a table at a small chalet up in the mountains." As she walked out into the parking lot she was amazed at how large it was. She really hadn't paid too much attention the night before. He guided her toward a bright yellow Vette. "That's it over there," he said, pointing to it, "That's our horse and carriage." He opened the door for her, and she climbed in. He had the top down in a minute. "This way you can enjoy the complete view and the fresh air of the Colorado Rockies." he smiled at her as he climbed in and buckle up.

They drove out on to the street and regardless of the traffic problem the woman at the airport had commented on; Tom seemed to drive through it at a remarkable pace with ease. "You look like you're sliding away. You know I'm a jealous guide and I demand all of your attention on me or nature as long as I'm your guide." He laughed, bringing her back to the present. The road was now speeding by and the grade was already starting up. The view was breathtaking. All of the lush green vegetation and the flame color of the hardwood trees showing all that fall would soon be hard upon us. The air was so pure she felt like she was on top of the world. The trees now were becoming closer together and they were such a vivid green. "They smell so good can almost taste them." She commented to Tom. He smiled. "Working up an appetite huh? We will be there in a few minutes, please don't eat the trees." She laughed at his sense of humor. The car turned into the lodge that looked as though it belonged in the Swiss Alps, with its steep roof coming down over the large windows, allowing a magnificent view for the guests. There was a quiet in the air; almost harmonic. The sounds of squirrels and birds being the only noise, except for the wind blowing through the pines. It is so tranquil it makes you feel as if life stands still. "I don't mind sharing you with nature." He slid his arm around her waist and started walking up the stairs.

As the door opened into the lodge she smelled the aroma of fresh biscuits and bacon and realized how starved she was. It was almost 10 o'clock now. They were seated at a table near the windows. "It's not too crowded this time of year but wait until the snow comes and the slopes open. You can't even get a table then. I much prefer this time of year when you don't have to fight the crowds." said Tom. She looked at him realizing that he must have been here before; maybe several times. "But I thought you said you lived in Houston?" She said. He laughed then. "I do. My father owns the Sky Lodge up at the top along with several other companies; so he sends me up periodically to check on things. The upkeep, the managers, the customer's satisfaction, improvements, things like that. When I first went into law Dad was pretty mad. He wanted me to take over his businesses and he couldn't understand why I was interested in the legal aspects of business. But, now that I am back with him to help him build his empire he's mellowed out some. He knows I like to ski so he sends me up here every time he thinks I need a break. This time he sent me because there is this oil well heiress who has had her claws out for me for some time that is back in town. The best way to avoid trouble with her folks and their invitations is to ship me out of town on business. Dad will give them his apologies. Men understand business before pleasure, so Dad won't lose a long-time friend." He smiled. "Looks like I have been hogging center stage. Tell me about Yakima. All I know about it is about a law case where the Indians were suing the Government over some treaty and water rights."

"It's really very pretty country to a farmer's eye. It is actually two vast basins." She was interrupted as the waitress set down their eggs, hashbrowns, bacon, with fresh made biscuits in a basket and refilled their coffee cups. She continued as the waitress left. "It is separated by the Yakima River, which is fed by the Cascade snow run off. The Cascades shelter the valley from moist pacific winds so there are about 300 sunny days a year. The soil is rich with volcanic ash so with proper irrigation the farmers can produce twice the yield per acre than the average farm. The valley leads the nation in apples, mint and hops. The valley is so green and the desert commences to rise up into the low rolling hills with sagebrush. As you come out on the top it is called Horse Heavens. Wheat fields run for as far as you can see in all directions. It is very dry, but it grows on you. That is where I was raised." They had finished eating and Tom sat content to listen to her rambling on. She smiled at him and she felt as if she had known him all of her life.

He was a very good listener. He was surprised at her knowledge of the farm country where she had grown up. Most women would have talked about the local dress shops, and theaters instead of the country. She was definitely a one of a kind. Beauty, brains, and a certain innocence not seen too often any more. "Well, what would you like to do today? Go on up to the Sky Lodge and watch me do business, or go see the sites in town?" he asked suddenly. "How about if we go on up to the lodge and you can do whatever it is you need to do, then we can go back to town. Since I am going to be living here, I can see the town any old time." "OK." he said. Getting up and leaving a very generous tip he walked over and paid the cashier. They walked out into the crisp mountain air and headed up the mountain to the Sky Lodge.

Down deep inside she felt guilty for taking the day off because she had so much she had to get done and she had to report to work in one week. "I'd better pick up a paper when we get back to town." she said out of the blue. Tom looked at her and said "Remember; me and nature today. I will help you find a place tomorrow." She was glad she had met him. It was so easy to just sit back and let him make the decisions. He was so sure of himself. But wasn't that why she had wanted to move here in the first place? To learn to make her own decisions? Suddenly it bugged her that he was moving in on her freedom that she had worked so hard to gain. She had to calm down. Anyway he would be going back to Houston pretty soon. Relax she told herself and enjoy your new found friend; When he leaves you might not have anyone. She smiled at herself then; relaxing back into the comfort of the deluxe custom seats of the Vette. How dumb she thought; fearing the loss of her new found freedom just because a friend offered to help her. She had to control a sudden urge to laugh out loud. She would hate explaining herself to him. They were at the lodge and the slopes looked like giant bare roads cut through the timber. The lodge was huge and very cold looking without any guests.

As Tom went up the steps a middle aged lady said "Dan is out working on the Ski Cats; making sure they are all in good running shape." She looked at me smiling a warm friendly smile and Tom introduced us. "It is really boring around here this time of the year; just cleaning and waxing skis." she said. "We can talk over some coffee while Tom and Dan talk shop." She turned when Tom had disappeared and walked back into the restaurant. She wanted to know all of the latest news. "I never get out of here except maybe once or twice a year to go pick up supplies. Usually Dan has those delivered, so I'm always glad to see another woman. Except for the skiing season there are only men here, and they don't like to talk much. Of course young Tom is an exception. He always has time to talk to everyone. You know you're a very lucky lady; getting Tom to set his eyes on you. A lot of girls would pay plenty for that chance. "Marge, you don't understand. Tom and I are just friends. That's all either of us wants." "Well, maybe you." Marge replied. "I've known Tom since he was a small boy and I know that look in his eyes when he looks at you is more than just a friend. But, if you insist, who am I to jump to conclusions." She liked this girl and if Tom wanted her to think they were only friends, then she wasn't going to get on his bad side. Marge had seen his eyes go cold for people before. She cherished the warmth of his eyes and she didn't ever want to be the recipient of one of his cold looks.

Tom and Dan entered the room and Marge was on her feet getting two more cups of coffee. "Shar this is Dan; Marge's husband. Dan this is Shar McCoy; my country bumpkin." Tom said and he smiled warmly at her. She knew that the nickname was to help her be accepted by Dan. She smiled back as she reached out and shook Dan's hand. Tom said "I'll take my coffee in the office. I need to get to the books if we intend to get out of here at a decent hour." Marge took Shar on a tour of the ski slopes. It was interesting; all of the things that went into getting the mountain ready for the season that Shar had never even thought about. All of the work in keeping the slopes cleared and the chairs and T-bars maintained. Also the roof and chimneys cleaned. The pump house and all of the equipment. It took them a couple of hours as Marge explained how everything was done to keep it up. "That doesn't include all of the work to get rooms ready for our overnight guests. When the season starts they hire a full crew; from bartenders to housekeepers to instructors. All we do then is make sure everyone else does their work." They were going up the stairs to the lodge and Marge told Shar "The office is the first door on your left; just go on in. I need to go start lunch. Let me know if you two will be staying."

Shar opened the door quietly trying not to disturb Tom, but he was just closing the books and putting them in the file cabinet. He smiled at her with a look of complete adoration in his eyes. "If the afternoon was a complete bore, I promise I'll make it up to you the next time we come up." he said. The slopes are a lot more fun with snow on them." She laughed, dropping her shield. He caught her by surprise. Two large steps and he was around the desk, grasping her by the shoulders, gazing down into her eyes. He frightened her. This was a side of him she hadn't seen yet. The hands on her shoulders were too tight. She knew it was too late to run. "Damn you," he breathed. "A man could drown in those eyes of yours if he wasn't careful." She thought he was going to kiss her; then he released her so quick she almost fell over. Trying to catch her balance, she reached out and grabbed his arm. He had half turned; then he spun around, reading her wrong, and pulled her to him placing light kisses all over her hair and moving down over her eyes, her cheeks, and then his mouth was searching for a response she could not give. Then, holding her at arm's length, stopping as suddenly as he had begun, he said "You did that intentionally didn't you? You enjoy making me beg for a response. I swear next time it will be you begging; not me. I'm a proud man and not even you with your innocent front will make me beg. And to think I fell for it...at first. It's probably pretty funny to you; so have a good laugh. I think it is past time we were getting back."

Shar was hurt by his accusations. She didn't ask for him to act like that. She realized, however, that to try to explain how she really felt would only make matters worse. So leave him a little pride. What would it do to him to know how wrong he had read her.

Marge was really surprised when Tom went in and said their goodbyes for them. The look in his eyes. "Did we make a mistake in the books?" she asked. "No." Tom snapped. "I'm just tired and I want to get back and make out my report. Better hurry I'd hate to waste any of Shar's precious time. She has a lot to get done." Then he remembered the promise to help her tomorrow. Well, he wouldn't break his promise, even if he were miserable all day. Who knows; maybe I could even make her miserable too. Now that might even be interesting, he thought to himself.

CHAPTER 3

S har sat waiting in the car looking out over the beautiful mountains, and thinking of the fun they had had just that morning. Why did men always have to bring sex into a relationship. I was perfectly happy to just be friends. Why couldn't he just treat me like another man. That way there wouldn't be any complications. She had decided to tell Tom, when he came back out, that it had nothing to do with him. That it was her that had the problem. That she just wasn't ready for a relationship of any kind other than just a platonic friendship. But, as he came walking up to the car he looked as if nothing at all had happened. He slid into his seat and pulled the car around to head out toward town.

"Tom." she stammered. "Yes my love!" he said with such sarcasm that you could feel ice in his voice. "Back there in your office. I just want to explain." "Don't bother." he said. "Forget it. I have." and he smiled a cold hard smile that sent chills up her spine. "That is unless you want an encore." She blushed. "No that isn't what I want." she said, and stared out the window. The drive up there had seemed so short, but on the way back it seemed like an eternity. Her mind was so confused. Half of it wanted him to hold and comfort her and the other half wanted to get as far away as possible.

It was almost 4:30 when they arrived back at the Hilton. Tom looked at her as he parked the car and said, "Don't forget to pick up a paper. Circle the places you like and we can run around tomorrow and check them out." He looked and sounded as if they had had a perfect day. She couldn't believe the way he had recovered so quickly from the afternoon. It was almost as if there were two completely different men in one body. One hard and passionate; the other soft and friendly. She was sure she liked the latter of the two, but wasn't sure she could control the first one. It was definitely a masculine and demanding personality. He walked her into the lobby, went to the desk and bought her a paper. Handing it to her he said, "Your work is cut out for you. Sweet dreams! See ya in the morning."

He got off on the second floor and walked briskly down the corridor. Shar didn't know if she felt sad or relieved that he hadn't wanted to eat dinner with her tonight. What do you expect? she thought. He's been with you all day and he promised tomorrow. Can't you even manage one lonely dinner? She thought of the way this man had made her doubt her feelings, and to her dismay she realized that she wanted him to hold her and comfort her again as he had the night before, when he had kissed her lightly on the forehead. I must be going stark raving mad she thought to herself as she shut her door.

Looking around her room she decided to set at the desk and get to work at finding an apartment. At least a two or three bedroom one as she had decided that she wasn't the kind of person to live alone. Maybe she could get a roommate or two who either worked at the company with her or went to school, or better yet just meet someone with their own lifestyle, completely separate from her own. There were quite a few ads for roommates wanted so she decided to circle all of those that were females, then mark out the ones that were on the wrong side of town. She didn't want to have to drive to far to work. Even though she had had plenty of practice driving around Yakima in the winter; she didn't like driving in the snow. If she couldn't get one in the right area she would just have to get the place, then advertise for roommates. So she set out to circle the interesting ones. She called and crossed out the ones no longer available. That left five possibilities. It was almost 7:30 so she thought she might as well get dressed and go down to dinner. Then she remembered she would have to set alone so she ordered it to be brought up to her room. She decided to call her folks to let them know everything was going alright. They would be happy that she had decided to have a roommate. They had always said it is safer for girls in numbers. She called and let it ring. It rang five times. She was just getting ready to hang up when she heard the faint hello of her mother's voice. "Hi Mom. This is Shar." "Is everything OK?" her mother asked hastily. "Yes, of course mom. I just wanted to call and say hi, and see how things are there." "Just fine Honey. We want you to get you a car. A good one that you won't get stranded in." her mom replied. "I will mom, as soon as I can afford it." "No we will pay for it. Just find what you want and let us know how much to send." Shar knew her mom and Dad would be hurt if she refused them this, so she promised tomorrow she would go look as soon as she was through house hunting. She laughed because her mom sounded so happy. "Say hi to Dad and I will call you tomorrow." Shar hung up and waited lying across her bed with her head hanging over the edge, looking at the world upside down like she used to do at home. Suddenly there was a knock on the door. Shar started over to open it then remembered "Who is it?" she asked. "Your dinner." came the reply. She opened the door and a boy no more than 17 pushed a cart in uncovering a dinner fit for a king. She smiled at him. "Are you hungry? I hate eating alone." she said. "Actually I am," he said, "but I'll lose my job if I start eating on company time. You know what I mean?" She laughed. "Then I won't tell if you don't." and she picked up a shrimp and held it tantalizingly under his nose. He snapped it out of her fingers with his teeth so fast she didn't even have time to jerk it back. Then he smiled at her. "That should teach you not to tease a boy. He might turn out to be more of a man than you could handle." With that he turned and walked toward the door.

Shar thought of his tip, but decided she had better just let him go before she got herself_ into more trouble with her friendly nature. She could just leave it at the desk for him tomorrow. She ate her dinner on the terrace and then she put the cart out in the hall so she wouldn't be interrupted. She took a brisk shower, washed her hair and went to bed. She went right to sleep within minutes after she got in bed. It must be jet lag she thought just before dozing off.

She awoke the next morning as dawn was starting to come in over the surrounding hills. You could see the pink and gold clouds as the sun was warming the world. She breathed in the early morning air. It had such a fresh smell compared to the air later on in the day. She wondered how people could stand to sleep until 10 and miss it all. Then she showered and put on an ice blue suit. It matched her eyes and she wanted to look her best today. Who knows. She may never see Tom again. At least she wanted him to remember her looking like a lady.

She smoothed the skirt down over her hips spinning in the mirror to see the effect it had. Yes it did compliment her figure. She wore a pin stripe blouse that matched and the jacket was tailored to fit, and that it did. She looked as if she had just stepped off the cover of a magazine. She brushed her blonde hair till it shined, and decided to leave it cascading down around her face. She put the finishing touch to her long dark lashes and smiled; knowing what she would do to the heads of the opposite sex.

There was an unquenchable need that had never been there until Mark had so casually made her feel like a child. Now she needed desperately to feel like a woman. To know she was not a child anymore. She knew that by looking so good, it would give her the confidence she had missed the last couple of days. She turned; satisfied with her accomplishment and went down to breakfast.

All eyes turned her way as she walked into the breakfast bar and sat down. She ate her breakfast in deep thought. Tom wasn't here. Maybe he had changed his mind and went back to Houston. Maybe she would have to take a cab house hunting, and car hunting. She had almost forgotten the promise she had made her mom to get a car.

"How is breakfast?" The voice sounded familiar. She turned and there stood Tom, looking her over from head to foot. "Talk about the devil," she said. "I was just thinking about you and here you are looking over my shoulder." "I hope the thoughts were good ones." he said. "No. I was thinking you were probably going to stand me up." His face dropped as if she had just slapped him. "Is that what you think of me? That I'm such a liar that I wouldn't even show up after giving you my promise?" What a swell way to start the day she thought. Even my thoughts upset him.

"I'm sorry." she stammered. "I guess I really don't know you yet. After all, I have only known you one day and we had our differences then." "And we still do." he said sliding in next to her. "You look lovely today. Did you do your homework?" His attitude changed back to the friendly, happy-go-lucky Tom so fast that she was taken aback. She was still on the defensive and all of a sudden there was no opponent; only her friend. She explained her plans for the day as he ate, then they took off for the first place on her list. It was in a big old house that had been made into apartments. There were steps in the hall that took you up to the second floor. There was a musky mildew scent as she climbed the steps. She felt awkward knocking on the door, for she was already hesitant to live here. The girl who answered the door seemed friendly enough, but she was dressed in dirty clothes and a scroungy looking man, that made Shar's skin crawl, was lounging on a bean bag chair. "We'd be real glad to have you." the girl said, eyeing Shar up and down. Shar replied, "This isn't quite what I was looking for so we had better get going." "Well if you don't find what you want, come back." Shar was relieved to be back outside, and she was thankful for Tom being there.

The second place was nice enough, but she didn't feel that she would get along that well with the woman who lived there. If all else failed, she could give it a try. When she got out of Tom's Vette at the third place she knew she loved it. The house was setting back off of the road down a drive with trees lining both sides. The house was beautiful with its steep roof reaching almost down to the ground. It was a large estate that had been divided into three rentals; two on the second floor and one on the first floor. The girls she would be sharing with lived on the first floor. It was as charming on the inside as on the outside. There were three bedrooms, a large kitchen, dining and front room with one whole wall a rocked in fireplace. There was a den, and it was furnished with a country autumn floral couch and rocking love seat. The tables were oak with tinted glass. It was very quieting on one's nerves.

She immediately liked Beth. She was warm and friendly with light brown hair curling around her face. Her eyes were a deeper brown and lit up when she smiled. She was short. Only about 5'4" and small boned. She was really pretty in a quiet sort of way.

Tom was comparing her to Shar and thought she looked like a quarter horse next to an Arabian. Shar was a little over spirited and Beth so very calm. He had to smile at his own comparison of the two girls. This would be a good place for Shar. Beth could keep her under control. It wasn't that he doubted Shar's ability to control herself, but he wanted her protected against her own naive ways, and Beth looked mature in city ways. His thoughts were interrupted as he heard Shar say, "I'll take it If you'll have me." Beth said, "It's fine with me and I'm sure you will get along fine with Megan my other roommate." "Great!" Shar replied. "I will pick up my things from the motel and move in tomorrow, if that's alright." "Sure." Beth said. Shar wrote out a check for the rest of the month and Beth gave her a key. "Feel free to come on in if I'm not here when you get here.

All of the tenants use the pool and the tennis courts. Do you play?" Shar answered "Yes." "That's great!" said Beth. "Now I won't have to pester Megan into it all of the time. Sometimes I'll bug you," she laughed. Shar laughed too and said, "If it isn't the other way around."

Tom and Shar walked out to the car. Tom looked pleased. "You couldn't have found a better place if you had looked all month." he commented. "Yes it's perfect!" she said, sitting back in the seat and thinking how well everything had gone since she had arrived. She was surprised when Tom pulled over in front of a small shop. "Lunch." he said. "This place has the best Italian food." They walked in off of the street. It was cool and dark with red and white checkered curtains and table cloths. The tables were all set with plain white coffee cups and red napkins. It had an aire all its own; very home like. He ordered salad and lasagna for them both. It came with French bread and it was delicious. Shar ate too much. She decided that she should have a light dinner to make up for all of the calories she was eating. They walked out of the shop into the late afternoon. It was really nice being escorted by Tom she decided at the way everyone looked at them and smiled; the men acknowledging his superiority; the women a little envious. She smiled back enjoying Tom's hand on her elbow.

They walked up to a flower shop set up on the sidewalk. Tom picked out a half dozen red roses and said, "Have these wrapped." Shar thought they were for someone else; then he handed her the box and said "These will look lovely in your new living room." She smiled. "You're too much." she replied reaching up and giving him a kiss on the cheek.

They were back at the car. He opened her door and went around and climbed in. "I'll take you to look for a car tomorrow, you won't need one tonight any way." They drove around looking at the sites for a while then they went back to the hotel. "Would you like to go dancing after dinner?" he asked. "Yes. That sounds nice." Shar replied. "Dress up!" he said. "I want to show you off tonight. Even if I don't know the people I'll be showing you off to." He smiled that infinite smile of his and Shar knew she would do her best to look good for him.

She showered and brushed her hair till it shined. Then she decided to curl it with her curling iron on the ends. Taking a comb decorated with crystals in the shape of a butterfly, she pulled her hair up on one side to expose the sensitive nape of her neck. She selected a white evening gown that she had bought for her junior-senior prom. It was long with a slit up one side to reveal her leg almost from the thigh down. The rayon fabric made it cling in all of the right places. It had been fitted to reveal her small waist; and

the plain white dress with small diamond studs in her ears gave her a look of pure elegance. She put a light touch of eyeshadow on, fixed her lashes, put a light blush on her cheeks, and put on frosty pink lipstick and nail polish. She slipped into her heels and sprayed white rain (her favorite perfume) on her wrist and neck dabbing a little bit at each pulse point. She was ready.

All of her efforts were rewarded. when Tom picked her up. With a low whistle he said, "I don't know if it will be safe to turn you loose on the public. Maybe I should just order the food brought up here and keep you all to myself." She smiled, knowing she had pleased him.

He was wearing a black tux with white ruffles. He was the perfect picture of masculinity. The jacket was tailored to fit his broad shoulders and slender waist. She could picture his chest muscles rippling under the ruffles. She had to tell herself to keep her mind on the evening instead of the man. There was something about a man in a tux she decided that excited her. Maybe, because in farm country you never see that; A night out means clean blue jeans and a western shirt. Maybe a tie if you're lucky. Wow! Was he good looking! She would have to concentrate to keep her mind on the things that were being said. She didn't want to encourage Tom in any way and chance another fight like up at the ski lodge. No way did she want to go through that again. She liked his less dominant side where everything was safe and warm.

"We are going to a special place where everyone there will be someone. Doctors; Lawyers; Big business men, a place where a princess like you should have her season started." She smiled at his English joke. As they walked up the stairs she felt like a princess walking into a castle. There were fountains of water changing their sprays and colors all the time on both sides of the walk and beautiful flowers cascading down from hanging baskets. They were surrounded by ladies in diamonds and furs

21

and gentlemen in tuxes. The chairs were all white rod iron with plush padded seats and backs. The tables were white with dark tinted glass. The lighting came from dark tinted glass features that had various shapes and propelled from ceiling to floor. It gave a shadowed effect. There were small candles in tinted fixtures in the center of each table making each one a private retreat. In the middle of the room and sunken down was a dance floor dividing the room. There was a piano bar over to the right of it and a stage at the front where a performer was singing a love song. This was by far the most beautiful place she had ever seen. Tom ordered her dinner for her as the menu was in French. Although she had taken French in high school, she wasn't at all sure of what all of the dishes were.

The food was excellent and she said "If you keep this up I'll probably weigh 200 pounds by the time you go back to Houston. I was going to have a light dinner to make up for the lasagna at lunch." "There will be plenty of time to diet after I leave." he said. "A working man needs good food and you know how I hate to eat alone. Besides we will work it all off after we eat unless you turn me down on the reason we came here. After all; it was to dance and show you off. I can't do that in this booth." He smiled at her and she smiled back. He was slowly losing his self-control as he gazed into those pools of ice blue. The fire was starting to burn inside and he had to fight the urge to grab her and ravish her right where she sat. There should be a law against girls looking so damned tempting he thought. His hands burned to touch her flesh and feel her body arch against him. He knew how great it would be to take her in his arms and smother her with kisses until she ached for him the way he ached for her; but he knew that would have to be later. Now he had to conquer her first in public. "Your eyes are giving me goose bumps" she stammered, trying to get him to stop that stare that was penetrating her very soul and making her very aware of the man on the other end of it. "Shall we dance then and quit staring?" "Sure anything beats that." she replied. No sooner had the words left her lips than she was sorry she hadn't picked them better. "Is that permission for me to do anything?" He smiled. "No" she blushed which made him smile even more. They were at the dance floor. He put an arm under hers and the other around her waist to help her down the steps to the floor; then he spun her into his arms. She felt so warm. He could feel her hot flesh through the thin dress. He lowered his head and kissed her lightly on the neck. She didn't know how to stop him without making a scene so she just followed his steps. The music flowed leaving her every nerve exposed to his tantalizing aroma and kisses she was starting to enjoy and the feel of his taught body drawn a little too close for casual dancing. She could feel that she was doing as much to him as he was to her. He was a superb dancer and he never missed a step.

She was glad when the band stopped for a break. She needed one to regain her composure. What was she letting this man do to her? She had to get ahold of herself. When they got back to the table she excused herself to go to the powder room. As she opened the door she saw the color that desire had brought to her cheeks. They were flushed from the temperature of her own blood. She knew it would take every ounce of will power she had or when this night was over she would no longer be a virgin. She had saved herself so desperately for her wedding night. She couldn't let this man ruin it. She could sneak out and take a cab home she thought; then pushed the idea out of her head as fast as it had entered it. That would be cowardice. She must learn to say no. She realized that the feelings Mark had first aroused in her were here to stay and running from Tom wouldn't kill them. She had to learn to control them. Damn she hated Mark for ever making her suffer this way...and the worst part was he didn't even know she existed. She washed her face with cool water and felt better. She went back to the table to find Tom waiting calmly as though nothing had happened. "How about another go on the floor?" She made apologies but said she was very tired. She knew she could not stand another half hour with his body melting her into his swirling her around the floor.

CHAPTER 4

They drove home in silence and Tom walked her to her room. She unlocked the door and started in, Tom caught her by the arms closing the door behind him with his foot. She stared up into his eyes, knowing by the passion there what was next but before she could protest his mouth took hers hot and demanding. She had no will power left to resist the response his lips demanded. She longed to do as they asked. Putting her arms up around his neck she let her lips respond to the passion that had been building continuously inside her. Her fingers entangled in the curls on the back of his neck. She pulled his head down harder; against her will. "No. No." She grasped for control. "Yes. Yes." he moaned, his breath hot against her skin. "You want me as much as I want you. Admit it." She had to think fast. There would soon be no stopping; for as they were kissing Tom had picked her up and was headed toward the bed. "OK. OK. I admit it. I want you." she whispered.

Tom released her letting her fall backward onto the bed. He laughed, "Next time! You beg. I love to hear you so docile." He went to the door, turned, winked, and smiled; then pulled the door shut softly behind him. She lay there staring at the ceiling, wanting to cry. He was the first man she had ever been willing to surrender to completely and he had laughed at her. She could kill him! The tears streamed down her cheeks. She took off her dress and threw it at the closet. Then from past training went and hung it up.

She couldn't control the tears. Why was she so upset? Why were her feelings so mixed up? Did she love this man? Or was she mad at herself for displaying her own passions so frivolously that he could play with them? She just knew that he had to be the most infuriating man she had ever known. Lying on the bed a jeer went through her head. First he wants you; then he don't; when he has you; then he won't. She thought back to the days when she used to jump rope and make up little sayings; but none were as realistic as that one, and it wouldn't leave. She cried herself to sleep.

The next day she got up and packed her things. One way to prevent the night before from reoccurring was to check out and move into her new found safety in numbers. She knew that there she would be more cautious because of Beth and Megan.

She went down to breakfast and Tom was sitting in the lobby. "Good morning sleepy head." he said. It was almost 10 o'clock. "I packed." she said. "Oh. I was wondering why you slept so late. I attributed it to you not getting to sleep too soon after I left. I must have lost my charm. Oh well, I can't win them all." He smiled a knowing smile that showed her he knew the affect he had left on her. Oh how she hated him with that pompous look on his face.

They went to several car lots after breakfast. She finally decided on a front wheel drive Izuzu, as they handle better in the snow. It was silver with grey interior. She had all the extras; air conditioning; a stereo; extra speakers; custom seats; and wide tires installed. Then she wrote them out a check and asked them to hold it until the following day so her parents could deposit that amount into her account. Sure they said. It's not often that someone comes in and pays cash for a car.

Shar was glad to have it, but that made her free from imposing on Tom. Now that she had her own car he wouldn't have to help her move. She wondered how soon he would be going back to Houston, and if he would ever come back and see her again. Doubts of their relationship were crowding her thoughts. They were interrupted by Tom. "If you don't like it we can look around some more." "Oh, I love it." Shar said. "My mind was on other things." "Are you disappointed that the extras you want will take a few days to install? We can put a rush job on it if you like miss." said the sales manager. "No. That's fine. Take the whole week if you need to. I'm in no hurry." She replied, realizing that he had just solved her problem.

Tom was quiet driving back to the Hilton. Shar had to know what was bothering him. The look in his eyes had been distant all day. She wondered if it had something to do with the night before. "Is something wrong Tom?" she asked after several minutes had gone by. "Yes and no"; he replied. "I have to go back to Houston tomorrow. My dad called last night. Seems they need my legal advice on a project he's getting into, so

I can't stay longer. I will have to leave early tomorrow. And the no is I'm glad you are all settled in so I have an address and phone number where I can reach you."

He pulled off the road and reached over and pulled Shar into his arms; kissing her lightly on top of the head. "Your hair smells so good," he said. "I want to remember you like this." Shar was frightened at first. Afraid that he would upset her emotionally as he had done the night before, but he just held her close in a comforting way. "I will miss you!" he said. Then as if not to lose control, he started the engine and pulled back onto the road. "We can pick up your stuff and get you settled in then have dinner. I have a lot to do tonight like put my car in storage and pack so I will have to drop you off back home early." "When will I see you again? She asked. "Maybe November; if I can wait that long." He laughed. "Make it a date in your date book." She smiled. That was three months away, but at least she would see him again. It only took her a few minutes as she had everything packed. She checked out and a doorman brought her luggage down, and put it in Tom's car. They pulled out and headed for her new home. She was pretty excited, but the thought of Tom leaving put a damper on her excitement. Tom was talking away about the place he lived, but Shar wasn't really listening. She was thinking of all of the things that had happened to her during the past week and wondered what lay ahead in her future.

Shar entered her room with her small suitcase. Tom had the two larger ones. It was a large white room with a double bed. There were light blue curtains drawn open to show the beautiful view of the garden. On the left of the window stood a large old dresser with a mirror inlaid in hand carved wood. It had nine drawers and a matching night stand stood on each side of the bed. The room was furnished, but she would need to get a lamp and a clock right away she thought; And sheets and blankets. She hadn't thought to bring those. There was sculptured high-shag carpet on the floor in a mixture of tans and browns and a large walk in closet. There was an adjoining bath with a sunken tub and shower. Very nice she thought. I need towels and wash cloths to and also soap. These things hadn't crossed her mind. Maybe Tom wouldn't mind stopping to shop tonight before dinner. She sat down on the bed looking around.

"Tom" she said. "What?" He said, looking back at her from where he had been looking out the window. "There are several things I need tonight. Would you mind taking me by the mall on our way to dinner? I need sheets, blankets, towels and wash rags; things like that." she said. "Don't you mean wash cloths?" he asked. "You know what I meant." she said blushing. He smiled and said, "I will take you shopping because I wouldn't be able to sleep imagining you here in your night gown without any covers to hide under." "How do you know I wear a night gown?" she teased back. "Because I can't imagine you being that uninhibited, yet." he stated. "What is this yet bit?" she asked. "Well someday yes, but now no." He caught her arm. "Let's go! This conversation is playing with my imagination and this isn't the safest place to be teasing a man in case you didn't know." She blushed timidly; "I never even thought," she stammered. "You're going to have to start thinking. I won't be here to watch out for you starting tomorrow. So start thinking! OK? I sound like your father now." he said shaking his head. She laughed and thought if he only knew her dad he would realize how different they were.

They were almost to the mall. She had decided to go with brown for the bath and blue for the bedroom. When they entered Sears she went straight to the linen department and picked out two sets of sheets with pillow cases to match in a blue and flowered pattern; a blue cotton blanket and a blue bed spread. Then she grabbed a couple of throw pillows; one blue and brown and the other blue. She picked up four bath towels; four hand towels; eight wash cloths; a bar of soap; a digital radio alarm; and a lamp that was crystal with a white shade, that would go with anything. She handed the sales lady her charge card and had it put on it; all except for the throw pillows. Tom insisted on paying for them. "I want you to think of me each time you make your bed and one way to insure that you do is to buy your pillows for you. See my motives are purely selfish." He laughed, bumping her on the head with one of them. They lugged it all out to the car and loaded the trunk and behind the seats.

CHAPTER 5

They had a pleasant dinner at a local hamburger shop at her request. She felt guilty for keeping him so long when she knew he had to pack and get ready to leave in the morning. When they pulled up in front of her house, Tom got out and opened the door for her. He loaded her down with stuff and got the rest out of the trunk. She got the door open; no one else was home now. They carried it into the bedroom and dumped it on the bed. Shar put the lamp on the nightstand and plugged it in. Tom just stood and watched her putting things in their right places. Then he took the radio out and put it on the other night stand while she hung towels in the bath and put the rest in a drawer. All that was left was the bed. She moved the sacks and put the blue sheets in a drawer. She took the floor set out of its package and went over to the bed. Tom went to the opposite side and helped her make the bed. She was beginning to worry about what he might be waiting for. She was very nervous by the time they got the spread on. Tom tossed the two throw pillows on the foot of it, turned and said "Now this looks liveable." She looked around satisfied with the effect of it. "It's missing something." she said. "I'll be right back!" She walked into the kitchen and picked up the vase or red roses he had gotten for her and brought them back into the room. She smiled at him and placed them on a washcloth she had spread out on the dresser. "Perfect!" she said, turning to see the warm smile on his lips and the satisfied look in his eyes. She was glad that she had thought of them because she really hadn't thanked him properly for them when he gave them to her and this would be as good a time as she would probably get. "Thank you for being so thoughtful." she said. "I really am going to miss you. You've been a terrific friend." He mimicked her in a high voice, "You've been a terrific friend." Walking toward her, his eyes turning hard, he said "I'll show you what a terrific friend I am." He grabbed her roughly and threw her back onto the bed.

"Don't fight it." he murmured in her ear as he started to nibble on it. Putting both of her arms together above her head and holding them with one hand he continued to let his other hand explore. He kissed her cheeks and her eyes then his mouth was on hers hard and demanding. She couldn't help responding to his touch and he released her hands. He raised up on one elbow. "Is this your first time?" he asked. "Yes," she said pulling him back down not wanting him to ever leave. "Damn," he swore half under his breath. He got up and went out the door closing it softly behind him. She realized Tom was gone and she started to cry. She fell asleep still laying across her bed in her clothes. She awoke several hours later; she was freezing. She wondered for a second where she was, then she remembered.

She got undressed and showered; put on her night gown and went to bed. Unable to sleep she lay there wondering if God had anything to do with the way she hurt at the thought of her loss of control where Tom was concerned. Would she ever get over him? Would she feel like this every time she thought of him?

Her eyes were bloodshot, swollen, and puffy the next morning from all of the crying and lack of sleep the night before. She had to get on with her life. Tom had gone out of it as fast as he had come into it she thought. She wet a cloth with cold water and laying it over her eyes she lay back down on the bed. She squinted her eyes hard under the cloth. There was a lump in her throat that made her feel like her chest would burst if she held it back. She had to stop this or she would be here all day. She got up and dressed in white shorts and a blue and white striped top. Pulling on her tennis shoes she thought this morning I will con Beth into some tennis. I need to get rid of my anxieties and put my emotions to rest. The best cure for that at the moment would be physical exercise.

Rummaging through her things she came up with her tennis racket and walked into the kitchen. Beth sat at the table drinking orange juice. Across from her was the most beautiful girl Shar had ever seen. She was only about five feet tall but her bones and frame were so delicate it gave you the impression that she was a porcelain doll. She had long dark hair almost to her hips. Her skin was a cream color and she had a slight tilt to her eyes. She smiled radiantly at Shar, exposing her teeth so white they looked like pearls. Her eyes were very dark and you could tell by the sparkle there that she loved and thoroughly enjoyed life and all that it brought.

"Megan this is Shar. Shar this is Megan." said Beth. The two girls shook hands. "Glad to meet you." Shar said with a friendly smile. "Likewise" said Megan. "You look like you will fit right in. Pull up a chair. Want some tea or some juice? Beth has been hounding me to play her a game this morning, but I really need to get down to the shop. I have to open up this morning the other girl called me and she is sick." "That's too bad." said Shar. "Wait until Beth runs you to death on the court and you'll see why I am glad to get away. She smiled at Beth and Shar could see the close friend ship that existed between them.

"See ya later" said Megan picking up her tea and finishing the last swallow. She washed out the cup and put it in the dishwasher. "Maybe this weekend we can get better acquainted" she said as she left.

Shar drank her juice and walked out to the tennis court with Beth. The air was crisp even though the sun was shining. "What are your plans for today?" asked Beth.

"I thought I would walk down and check out where I will be working, and maybe the college and town this afternoon." said Shar.

"Well, I have to be at work at 8, but if you'd like to you could meet me for lunch. I work on the corner of Colorado Blvd and 2nd. Meet you out front at 12 if you want me to."

"Sure. That sounds great," Shar replied, knowing that it was going to be easy liking Beth.

Shar's body responded to the excitement of the game and before she realized it she was having fun and laughing. Beth was good and it was a challenge to beat her. They finished the set 4 & 6 with Beth ahead. Beth had to shower and get to work. "Want to do this again tomorrow?" she asked as they gathered the balls. "Sounds good to me", Shar said, looking forward to the following day with great anticipation.

After they had showered and changed Shar was looking for a cab in the phone book when Beth said "If you're ready I can drop you off on my way into town. I go right by the Flair Clothing Co." "Thanks" Shar said. "I am really excited to see it."

"Well, come on, let's go before I'm late," stated Beth.

They left and as they were drawing closer to where she would be working Shar wondered about the way she looked. Did she make the right decision in wearing the suit? She was starting to be nervous and have doubts about her self, well, it wouldn't matter if she had or not. She wasn't reporting to work today; only looking the plant over to see what she would be doing starting on Monday. Her stomach had a hollow spot as she opened the large entrance door. This was much bigger than she had anticipated. She had landed the job by sending in a design she had done herself and apparently someone had liked it, because they had replied in their return letter for her to report here on the second floor to work.

She went to the front desk when she discovered you have to have a security card to operate the elevator. She walked over to a desk where a lady sat reading a magazine. "Excuse me, but I came to report for a job I have here." Before Shar could explain what department, the woman looked at her with contempt in her eyes. "You girls are all alike; not a brain in your head. It's a good thing God gave you good looks." Shar was beginning to wonder what she had done wrong when the woman pointed to the elevator on the left and said "You go up in that one to the sixth floor. You don't need a card to work it. Go down the corridor to your right to room 633, take a chair and someone will help you."

As she entered the elevator, Shar wondered, how was I supposed to know that? They hadn't stated how she was to get into the building in her letter. She was wondering what had made the woman at the desk act so rude. She should have a few lessons in manners, Shar thought, smiling to herself as she stepped off on the sixth floor. She turned right. The woman's directions had stuck in her mind; Room 633. She didn't even want to have to go back down for seconds. Once with that woman was enough to last a life time. Shar was now standing just outside room 633. She opened the door and to her surprise there were about 15 other women setting in the chairs lining the walls. "You're almost late" one girl said as Shar came over and sat down in a chair next to hers. "Late?" Shar commented.

"You are here to work aren't you?"

"Yes of course if they need me," Shar answered, thinking they must be desperate to put her to work today, but she really wouldn't mind. She hadn't really made any plans that she couldn't break.

CHAPTER 6

er thoughts were interrupted by a little man wearing thick bifocals. He had a high squeaky voice and bald head. "All of you line up over here. Gene will show you where to change into your clothes." Shar looked down at her suit; wasn't it appropriate? Well, if they had to wear special uniforms here she wouldn't mind; at least it would save on her wardrobe expense. She followed the other girls into a large dressing room and each one was fitted by the tall slender woman with her hair in a French roll. Shar decided she must have been a model at one time by her grace and poise, and definite good looks even though she was probably in her late forties.

All of the dresses were of the same exact design. Aqua blue with white lace bordering the low cut V necks. Very revealing she thought, just to draw in. Also they were of such fine material you felt like you had nothing on, but to look in the mirror she looked like an innocent princess getting ready for her first ball. Then they were all rushed into a second room where men and women put new makeup on them exclaiming that hers just wouldn't do in the bright lights. Shar thought to herself, I guess I should just come to work in jeans and no makeup If they are going to go to all this trouble taking me all apart and changing me before I can start to design clothes. Maybe this was to get her into the mood to design for the rich. Who cares, it's fun being fussed over she thought. A man walked over to her. "Is this your first job?" "Yes," Shar said, "Is it that obvious?" "Well, just watch the other girls and act natural in front of the camera." he said. "You'll do just fine." Smiling he walked on. Shar looked at herself in the mirror and couldn't believe her eyes. She was beautiful. All of her hair was pulled up and over and curls cascading all over the other side. A string of miniature blue roses separated her hair and there were a couple floating about half way down in her curls.

She followed the rest of the girls out into a dark room with a big round bed and a make believe dinner set with a lit candle and one of the girls sat drinking champagne as a man took pictures. Across from her was a gentleman in a black tux. They stood up and walked off the set. "Next!" the man yelled and another girl went on to do the same scene while the man took up more film. This went on and Shar realized these were all models and they were doing some commercial or something. She realized she didn't belong here so she started to leave but found the door was locked. Walking up to the man with the squinty eyes she said "Excuse me, but I think there has been a mistake made." She was interrupted by him. "Mistake made? You think? We don't pay you to think! That is my department. You go sit down and keep quiet until you are through shooting. Mistake made. Ha! I don't believe the nerve of these models these days." "But" Shar stammered. He excused her saying "Go sit down; I don't have time to mess with your quibbles right now."

Shar sat back down and thought to herself, I will just set down; serves you right you dumb chauvinist if you waste your precious time and film on me. Shar decided she was going to enjoy this. He deserved it and after all it wasn't every day you could get a special film shooting at the expense of a chauvinistic, arrogant man. After all it's not my fault. I tried to explain, she thought to herself. Now that her mind was made up, she watched with more concern. If she was going to waste her afternoon here she might as well learn all she could.

Watching the other girls, she picked out things that looked good and things that shouldn't be done so when her time came she would know. She was excited but completely confident; for what did it matter if she goofed, he deserved it; but to her surprise the shooting went off perfectly and he sent her over to take some special shots on the bed. By now she was enjoying the camera man's attention and played it to the hilt. Giving him her most sensuous look down to her timid and free expressions. She was happy with her performance as she walked off and was escorted by Gene back to the dressing room where she put a check by her name signifying that the dress was turned in. Gene smiled at her and said "We'll be seeing you again I'm sure! You're a naturalist; you didn't look the least bit nervous." Shar smiled "I wasn't" Walking out the door she could just imagine old squint eye's face when he realized they had filmed someone not even on their staff. She had to laugh.

She got off on the second floor from the elevator. It was almost 3 she noticed by the clock behind the security desk. She had missed her lunch date with Beth, but she didn't regret it. When she told the other girls of her unusual day they could all have a good laugh. Men! She was glad there were none in her life right now. They were all so pompous.

"I am reporting for a job I am supposed to start Monday, but I thought if someone had time they could show me where I will be working and how to get in and fill out my W-2 forms and all that technical stuff today." He smiled at her. "With those looks and that hair-do, my first impression was that you were on the wrong floor. What job are you going to be doing?"

"I am going to be a designer apprentice to start out."

"Brains and beauty; a rare combination around here. Most of the looks go on up to the sixth floor, by passing us," he said.

Shar smiled thinking of the woman down stairs. No wonder they all wound up on the sixth floor she thought.

The man pushed the button on the intercom. "There is a young woman here. Says she's here to design. Do you have anyone free to sign her on and show her around?"

The woman's voice sounded hard and cold. "What's her name?"

"What's your name?" the man asked, releasing the button so whoever was on the other end wouldn't catch his error of incompetence, by being swept over by her good looks.

"Shar McCoy." she answered.

He pushed the button down again; "Shar McCoy." he stated. Then laughing he said into the intercom; "Maybe some relation to Ellie-May. She looks like an animal lover." The intercom clicked. Apparently the woman on the other end didn't appreciate his sense of humor.

Within seconds a tall dark haired man opened the door. "Miss McCoy? I'm Matt. Matt Parker." he continued putting his hand in hers; looking down into her ice-blue eyes. The fire burning with in them made him feel awkward and aroused. This was an unusual effect. This was one he knew he would have to avoid. He had been around plenty long enough to sense his own infatuation building; and one thing he knew for certain she was young enough to be his daughter.

He had a good build for a man of his age, with grey starting to make him look distinguished edging the temples of his hair line. You could tell by his manner and self-assurance that he had had a successful life. His clothes showed he had good taste and he wasted no expense in showing it. "Come with me." He opened the door for her. They went down a corridor with several offices on each side. There were people hard at the sketching boards in some and some were just sitting at their desks typing.

Shar felt a certain twinge of excitement surge through her veins at the thought that here in all this she had landed a job. They passed by an empty room and Matt paused a second. "This is where you will be working, with a designer named Carol. She will be your advisor for a while until we see how you work out. Advances here are all up to you. Seniority only counts according to your production. If you are good you can go to the top fast. Our only rules are you be polite and courteous to other workers. We frown on employees dating other employees other than just as friends. Any problems with employees or work your advisor can't handle, come see me, my office is at the end of the corridor. Any problems I can't handle I send on to Miss Davis. Hopefully she can. If not then Mark will, but believe me he hates to be bothered. Even with those blue eyes of yours, I would hesitate to go to him. He eats little girls like you for dinner." Smiling at the fear showing in her eyes he said "Come on; You probably won't ever be called into his office, unless you do exceptional work."

They had reached his office. He held a chair out for her. As she sat down he walked around to his side of his desk. Pulling open the file cabinet he handed her some papers to fill out. Mostly the questions were all routine. She hesitated once and looking up saw the look in his eyes as he sat with a pen in the corner of his mouth staring openly.

"Don't you have anything better to do?" she smiled.

"Not at the moment. Not anything I would rather do anyway." he smiled back and it made the skin on the back of her neck crawl. She knew he was enjoying letting her know that he would like nothing more than to physically take her. She realized if she was going to get along here, he was going to have to be set straight from the beginning. She couldn't tease this man. In fact, she would have to try to ignore any signals that weren't purely platonic.

"See ya at 8 o'clock Monday morning," he said. "You don't have to spend so much time on your hair. There is no one here to impress unless you have changed your mind and thought this was a good way to get into modeling."

"No; you're out of luck," she said. "Designing is the love of my life; not the camera."

"Well here is a security card so you can get in. Carol should be here Monday to show you the ropes."

She smiled. "He could be really nice when he wanted to."

She flagged a cab down and got into it. "Where to lady?" the cab driver asked.

"To any grocery market that is nearby. I'm not too familiar with this area yet." she commented. She had decided to do some grocery shopping. She felt funny eating there without paying for some of the food. As she walked up and down the aisles, she realized how little she knew about Megan and Beth. For all she knew, they might be vegetarians. So she picked up some fresh fruit and vegetables; a few cans of soup; some crackers and bread; yogurt; orange juice and milk. That should do for now. If they eat meat I can stop by again tomorrow and get some.

Shar stood fumbling with her keys, trying to get the door unlocked while holding two bags of groceries when Beth pulled in. "Hold on and I'll help." she said, running up to take a bag. Shar managed the lock with ease then.

"Why didn't you show up for lunch?" she asked looking at Shar. "Did you get lost?"

"No." Shar felt a little guilty at the hurt look on Beth's face. "I have a good reason though." So she told Beth of her day at the factory and Beth laughed. "I'd love to see his face when he sees the mistake he made now." They both laughed as they put away the groceries. "I didn't know if you two were vegetarians or not so I didn't buy any meat." "We're not." Beth answered, "But that's alright. We have plenty in the freezer. Usually we all go shopping on weekends together. That way we get food we all like, then we split the bill."

Meanwhile back at the office the film had been developed. Mark sat in his office viewing the finished product.

"Oh Mark darling I don't know why you spend hours here staring at all of those girls. When you have seen one you've seen them all." she stated. "If you are going to spend the entire night doing this I might as well go home." She pouted. Usually that would get her her way with Mark, but he was different tonight, and he looked at her with disgust.

"Go on home, but please shut up about it. I've had it up to here with interruptions today." he said putting his hand to his throat. "Can't you see I have a business to run?"

Priscilla was steaming. She was spoiled and didn't like anything that disrupted her plans. She stormed out and said, "You will pay for this Mark Flair. This is the last time I come begging you to go as my escort. You know the precedent that has at a party." She went out slamming the door behind her.

Mark smiled, knowing that she would call and apologize for her actions within the week. She always had and always would. He reached down and flicked the projector back on. It was important that he find just the right girl for this promotion as they were going worldwide with it.

The screen grabbed his attention. This blonde set the world on fire with her ice-blue eyes and an air of owning the world. The dress came to life and so did he. "That's her!" He jumped up grabbing the phone. He had to reach Ralph and get her to sign before someone else did. Where had he seen her before. He couldn't quite place her, but he knew he had seen her somewhere. Maybe it was just someone who looked like her a little he thought. Surely someone who looked like that, he wouldn't have let slip through his fingers. Not before he had sampled her anyway. He was well known for his affairs with pretty models and the rich beautiful women of his acquaintance. He had the opinion that God made women for men's enjoyment. He had never met a woman who didn't succumb to his charm, good looks, or money. So he went around using them one and all. The ringing was finally interrupted by a high squeaky "Hello, Ralph speaking."

Ralph. Where in the hell have you been? I thought the phone was never going to get answered."

"I just got home. I stopped by the store on the way. Sorry boss." Ralph squeaked.

"Well I need you to come back to work. There is a girl here in the pictures I have decided to go with for our campaign. I want her signed tonight, before someone else discovers her."

"Can't it wait until morning? Those modeling agencies don't like to be disturbed after hours?" asked Ralph.

"For what I'm willing to pay they had better learn to like it." Mark snapped.

Ralph said, "Be right there boss." He knew better than to argue with Mark when he was in a mood like this.

Ralph wasn't surprised at the one Mark had chosen. Next to her the other girls looked lifeless. There was a certain spark of life almost like fire in her eyes that turned a man's insides topsy-turvy.

"I remember her Mark," Ralph commented. "She is the one who tried to tell me how to do my job."

"From the looks of her you should have listened," Mark smiled knowing how much Ralph hated women to tell him what to do. "Well, get her found. Which agency sent her?" Mark asked.

Ralph checked his book. All of the other girls had their agencies listed right after their names, but she didn't. If that was the mistake she had been trying to tell him, Mark would kill him if he found out. So Ralph tried to be cool. He started calling all of the agencies that usually sent them girls. None of them had any record of her. Next he decided to call all of the girls who showed up. Maybe she just came with one of them, but again none of them had ever heard of her. Ralph was beginning to get nervous. What was Mark going to do when he found out that he had photographed a girl who hadn't even been sent over by an agency? Maybe she was even a spy.

CHAPTER 7

Before he would take the wrath he knew Mark was capable of, he would call every McCoy in the phone book. Surely he could find her that way. Again he tried to no avail. It was 11:30 at night and he was beginning to wonder if she even existed. He was getting tired. Maybe the hotels or motels he thought, so he called one after the other. It was already 1:30 in the morning; would he be here all night?

The voice at the other end said "Hilton Hotel; May I help you?" "Have you a guest there by the name of Shar McCoy?" he asked.

"No we don't," the lady replied. "She checked out of here yesterday, even though she had her room reserved until Monday. She was seeing that womanizer. You know; Tom Hinley? Well, the way they were looking at each other they probably decided to go get a place a little discreet; if you know what I mean. She chuckled; She loved the chance to put these rich people in their place.

Her tongue wagged on, but Ralph didn't have time to listen. He couldn't believe his fate. The Hinley's had just bought out one of their biggest competitors. So that was why she couldn't be found. Yes, she was a co-spy. Mark had to be told. She was probably on her way back to Houston to give away their new advertising campaign. I knew she was too smart to be a model. I just had that feeling.

It was almost 2:00 in the morning now. He hated to be the one to call Mark, but every second time was wasting, Mark would be even madder if he waited until morning to tell him.

The phone rang and rang. Finally, Mark's sleepy voice was saying "Ya; What time is it?"

"It's 2 a.m. but I thought you would want to know."

"Who the hell is this calling me at 2 in the morning to tell me what time it is. I swear if I find out I'll kill you; or whoever put you up to it." He slammed down the phone, and turned toward the wall. The phone was ringing again. Mark was really agitated now. He turned over and picked up the phone. He was fully awake now and his voice was as cold as ice. "May I help you?"

"Mark this is Ralph!"

"What is it Ralph?"

"I'm still at work Mark. That girl hid her tracks real good; but I found out she is a spy working for the Hinley Co. of Houston. You know the one that just bought out our biggest competitor? Well, she didn't put an agency by her name at the shooting; so I called them all. Then I called all of the McCoy's in the phone book. None of them had ever heard of her either. I'm not sure if that is even her real name. Then I started calling all of the hotels, and she checked out of the Hilton with Tom Hinley. The desk clerk left out nothing about how close the two of them were."

Mark was mad when the phone had interrupted his sleep. The first real sleep he had had in a week knowing that he had finally found the girl for his campaign had helped; but now he was outraged to have it thrown back in his face that he couldn't have her. And on top of that she was a spy for another man; his competitor!

If he could just get his hands on her now, he would wring her pretty little neck. No better yet; he would show her what a real man was like, and make her sorry she had ever dared to cross him. He hated traitors. If it were a man he would have him taken out and whipped. But, since it was a girl; one that made his mouth water just to see on film; he promised himself he would find her and make her pay! Pay for every dream and every want he had felt for her. "Can you find her and young Tom?" he asked Ralph.

"Well I can get our detective staff to put a couple of men on it tomorrow."

Mark stated; "I don't want a word of this to leak out. Do you understand?"

"Yes", stammered Ralph, "But why Mark?"

"Because I want that girl and I don't care what it costs me I am going to have her. Ralph I don't want her to know that I know she is a spy or I'll never catch her. I am going to set an example with her that will make the Hinley money very unappealing to any other young fool."

Ralph wondered if Mark had gone off the deep end, and if he might kill this beautiful young girl. He felt sorry for her innocence.

"I want every report on them turned in to me personally!" Mark stated. "Good work Ralph. Take tomorrow off."

Mark was unable to sleep. He decided that he would fly down to Houston tomorrow himself and talk to young Tom Hinley and find out where Shar McCoy had gone. He called the airport making reservations for the next flight out. He could be into Houston by 10 a.m. Then he could find this girl who had interrupted his life and made fools of his security system. How beautiful she was and clever too. He would have to watch his step not to reveal his real intentions.

As Mark walked up the steps to the office of Hinley Enterprise, he decided he would have to go by an assumed name. John Smith would have to do. That wasn't too unique; he would just tell them his name was John if they didn't ask for a last name. He would just say he was a friend of Toms. He almost stopped and went back as he reached Toms office, but he was determined to find this girl. He opened the door and it was quiet except for the sound of a typewriter. The receptionist looked up.

"Is Tom in today?" Mark asked.

"Yes, but he is busy. Do you have an appointment?"

"No. I wanted to surprise him." Mark said. "We're old friends. We go back a long way. Please don't ruin the surprise. I have flown a long way, not even sure if he would be here, only to see the look on his face when I walk in."

Mark was telling the tale with such a look of compassion in his eyes that the girl decided not to ruin his surprise. It would probably do Tom good to see an old friend. He had been so on edge ever since he got back from Denver. "Go on in." she told Mark. He shut the door quietly behind him.

"What can I do for you?" Tom said getting up and extending his hand across the desk to shake. Mark clasped it firmly. "My name is John and I have confirmed that you and Shar McCoy were very close at the Hilton in Denver and that she went with you when you left."

Tom stood there half smiling, for he knew the implications that this man was putting on the situation. "So you're John." Tom said smiling as he realized that this man had judged the situation between him and Shar as a threat. Maybe I do have a chance he decided, if someone else saw it this way. Just maybe. "Shar told me about you." Tom continued.

"She did?" Mark was taken aback. "What did she say about me?" he asked, wondering who this John was that he was supposed to be.

"Oh nothing much except that you two made a mistake in ever getting engaged. And that she was glad it was over so she could go on with her life."

"She did, huh?" Mark said coolly. "Well I want to know where she is!" he demanded.

Tom was enjoying having the edge on this man. He wasn't sure how Shar had managed to break off their engagement. This looked like a man who took what he wanted and asked questions later. If Shar hadn't given him her address, she probably knew she couldn't resist if he found her again. She had to have her reasons. He couldn't let her down and lose the only chance he had to win her heart. He looked Mark in the eyes; "If she wanted you to know, I am sure she would have told you. And if she wanted you to follow she wouldn't have bothered to cover her tracks." He tried to make it sound cold so that this man would go home or off to war or wherever he was supposed to be and give up on Shar. He was beginning to get a little discouraged, for this man looked like the type who would not give up. "Well," Tom said "Why don't you try to find her. I have several villas and she could stay in any one for as long as she likes and never show her face with all the servants to run for her." If he could only keep this John down here in Houston, Shar would be safe. He was playing with his jealous and speculating side now.

Try as he would Mark could not get an ounce of information out of Tom. Finally he gave up. He was boiling mad as he got off the plane in Denver. So far he had flown to Houston and back; spent about 1400 dollars on filming her; plus putting Ralph on overtime for 9 hours. It was adding up fast; what he was going to collect from her oversexed body. It might be worth it but he was beginning to doubt it. From the film he thought her the most beautiful girl he had ever set eyes on with her charm and innocence and sex appeal. But the more he found out about her the more he disliked her; dumping her man just to run with this Tom and his money. Then to stoop so low as to spy and steal other peoples' ideas that they had worked hard for. It wasn't as though the Hinley's couldn't afford to work for their own ideas. Right now he hated her and couldn't see how he could get any pleasure from her body. Maybe if she would cry and beg for him to stop he could enjoy the pain he could give her. He shook his head; no you have to keep calm and think this thing through. Mental pain hurts for a lot longer than physical pain.

He would sweep her off her feet and make her fall in love with him. Yes. That was a much better idea. Then after he had had her he could tell her that he knew the truth and dump her. That would be more in her ball park. To shatter her hopes and dreams the way she had done his. Not to mention pride. Yes; he thought to himself; that would hurt a lot deeper and a lot longer. Also he would serve Tom Hinley a dose of his own medicine in the process.

Mark smiled as he walked to his Porsche at the airport garage where he had left it. It was his only real love with its silver shining gleam. At least it was always faithful. Sliding in behind the wheel he felt a surge of reassurance. He loved the power of the car in his hands as he was cruising down the road toward home. He would have to wait until morning to find out if the detectives found out anything more while he was gone.

Turning into the drive he inserted his key; the gate opened and he drove through. The sight of home always gave him a lonely feeling; ever since the plane had crashed killing his fiancé and parents three years before. Now the only familiar faces here were the maids and butler. Only two maids and one butler had stayed on since no one lived here anymore other than Mark. There was really no need for a full staff. Mark walked up the huge marble steps stopping to look around out over the landscape. He hadn't realized how beautiful it was this time of year. As a matter of fact, he really hadn't taken time to look at it since his folks had died. He had hired a new gardener. The old one had wanted to retire after the accident. He said he just couldn't stand the place without them there. He had worked for them for 17 years. He had tried to talk Mark into selling and getting a place with less memories at first but his stubbornness kept him from doing it.

As he looked around at the trees in the moonlight and the big old house where he had grown up he was glad that he would have it to pass on to his son someday, if he ever had one. Why am I thinking this way tonight of all nights he wondered? He walked in the house discouraged, dropped his keys onto the night stand by his bed and sat down rubbing his hands through his hair. Why me lord? When I think I've got something I really want; why do you take it away? Flopping back on the bed he closed his eyes and fell asleep.

CHAPTER 8

Shar awoke; she was so excited at her first day of work. She couldn't eat so she drank a glass of juice. She wore a tan dress that had a full skirt and puffy sleeves. It was modest and pretty. She wanted to be confident yet not to over done for fear of putting off the other employees' friendliness. She did so want to make friends with the other employees at Flair.

She stepped into the elevator after passing the old witch at the reception desk with a smile. She felt so good she couldn't even stay mad at her today. She went to her office laughing at her memories of Friday, when she thought they were dressing her up just to design. The thought went through her head; What if she should bump into Ralph. By now he would have surely discovered the mistake he had made? Would he try to get her fired? No she would just explain that he wouldn't listen to her when she tried to correct the mistake before it went so far. Would they believe her? A new employee? Or would they believe him? He had apparently been here forever. Well, she would just have to do her best. Maybe her work could prove itself before anything ever happened over the incident.

Shar was at her office now. Carol was sitting at her table sketching. She looked up as Shar entered. "I'm Carol. You're Shar?"

"Right," Shar said, extending her hand to clasp the extended hand of Carol. Shar based a lot on first impressions and Carol was friendly yet impersonal. "Here are some sketching pads." said Carol. "If you need more the supply room is the first door on your left as you come on the floor. You might as well get started so I can try to pick apart what you do; or praise it and make any suggestions of my own that might help."

Shar had her own opinions of what would sell that weren't being created yet so she started to draw. She designed her clothes with a feminine look to them through full flowing skirts; V shaped necks; pleats; and pockets with handkerchiefs sewn in. She had a natural talent for style and before the morning had passed she had several sketches started of different styles and designs for Carol to go over. Carol was surprised at the talent and at the ease with which pictures seemed to form on the sketch pad for Shar. She was definitely productive and very good. Carol made a few suggestions as to color schemes and Shar taking her advice took her colored pencils and started to color them in.

There was a cantina in the building so Carol and Shar went there for lunch. Shar was starved but she had a salad; remembering all of the pasta and food of the previous week. Carol asked; "Got a boyfriend?"

"No not really." Shar answered, thinking of Tom.

"Well wait till you see Mark Flair, the owner here. All of the girls here have a crush on him, even though it is no use. He only goes with models. Word has it he only uses women to satisfy his urges, if you know what I mean? Watch yourself; you're pretty enough to be a model and he may mistake you for one and make a move on you." She smiled teasingly. "Not that I would mind if he used me, but you seem to sweet and innocent for a man as ruthless as him to play with and discard."

Shar was surprised at Carol's open ridicule of her employer. "How can you say that about him?" she said. "If you've never gone out with him. They're probably just rumors. No one could be that cold and besides if the models let him use them, then they get what they bargained for."

"Wow!" Carol said. "Sounds as if he's a friend of yours."

"No. I haven't met him yet. But I'm not going to judge the book by its cover."

Carol laughed. "Shar you are refreshing compared to the stuffed shirts around here. But, promise me you'll be careful if you ever do meet him."

Shar said, "I've handled my share of wolves, and in a lot more open environment than this out on the ranch."

Carol laughed again. "Yes I guess you probably have. Your youth just brings out my motherly instincts I guess."

Shar was beginning to forget the modeling episode. Two months had passed and she had been working very hard. A lot of her designs had been accepted and developed. Matt was standing at the door of her office. He said "Shar, your last design has been picked to start off the boss's new campaign."

Shar smiled, she got a lot of pleasure out of success. She had worked hard on that one and it pleased her that it had been picked. "Thanks Matt." she said still smiling.

"Don't mention it." he said." You may not be so thankful when the boss gets done with you."

"What do you mean by that remark?" Shar blurted out; looking at him questioningly.

"Oh just observation." he said with a lazy smile creeping onto his lips. "It's too bad you know. He tells us hands off then he takes whatever he wants to play with."

"Well, I'm not for the taking!" Shar said looking at Matt with a disgusted look on her face.

"We'll see." he said. "The Boss wants to meet this mysterious lady of both brains and beauty. Who knows; maybe he's met his match. I hope so for your sake Miss McCoy."

"When" she asked.

"All ready for his beck and call!" Matt replied.

"Well, I couldn't very well refuse to meet him under the circumstances could I? He is my employer."

"I see what you mean." he said. "I just hate to lose a good designer."

"Lose a good designer?" asked Shar. "What do you mean? Is he going to fire me? Did I do something wrong?"

"No! No!" Matt did laugh then. "You are so naive. I feel like I'm sending a lamb to the lion's den."

Meanwhile Mark was looking at the dress made from Shar's design. Perfect to the tee, and to think that spy had had the nerve to use the name of one of his own top designers to make her way into his company. He still hadn't given up on finding that girl; but his detectives had had a tail on young Tom Hinley ever since that day and he had not gone to her. Tom must think a lot of her to stay away from her to protect her, he thought. But some time somewhere he would goof. Mark was sure of that. The answering service interrupted his thoughts. "Shar McCoy here to see you, Mr. Flair."

Shar was nervous as she heard him reply "Well send her in." She knew that voice from somewhere but couldn't place it. The secretary went over and opened a door. "Right this way Miss McCoy."

It wasn't often that Mr. Flair had meetings with the staff in the designing department. Apparently it's her looks the secretary had decided. That was what Mark had called her here for.

Shar had on the same light blue suit that she had worn the first day to look over the building and she did look stunning with those matching aqua eyes. The secretary asked Mark "Is there anything I can get you?" for he was as white as if he had seen a ghost.

"No. That will be all Miss Flint you may go. Shut the door please." She went out closing the door behind her.

Shar was surprised that Mark Flair was the same Mark that had sat beside her on the plane. Now she understood everyone's comments. Be careful she thought remembering his rudeness. Oh, she didn't need to be warned against him and his arrogance.

"Miss McCoy." He caught hold of himself. The shock was well buried now. He smiled. Revenge was well overdue.

Shar smiled back. He couldn't believe the nerve of this girl. She had to be the best actress in the world. She didn't even look the least bit nervous. She must not even suspect we know, he thought.

Shar was beginning to get nervous. He had just been sitting there looking at her like a cat about to pounce and all he had said was her name. Shar thought maybe he was trying to remember where he had seen her. He must have forgotten the plane trip. "Are you trying to remember where you met me?" she asked.

"Am I supposed to have met you before Miss McCoy? Surely I wouldn't forget a face like yours."

Shar just sat there not knowing what to say. If she told him where, that would bring back the flight and that he thought her still wet behind the ears. "No" she said at last; "But a lot of people think at first that they have. There must be someone that looks like me out there somewhere." She tried to think fast. "No I don't think so Miss McCoy. When God made you he made you one of a kind."

How many times Tom had said that to her, she thought, but it sounded like a sneer coming from Mark. "Why do you work in design with looks like yours? You could be a top fashion model you know."

Shar said, "I suppose, but the love of my life is designing, not modeling."

Mark was trying to decide what made this voluptuous girl tick. All of the girls he knew would die for a spot in front of the camera, and it is quite obvious that sitting in the designing room and being a spy could very well be done by even the homeliest of all. Although having looks might have its deterrents. He had to give Tom credit for that had been clever. "Do you like working for us?" He looked straight across the desk into those pools of fire.

"My work wouldn't be good if I didn't enjoy doing it." she said smiling. She was clever Mark thought. What a way to avoid giving a straight answer. "And these designs you have been handing in have been your work?" He had stood up and walked toward the window. He turned raising his eyebrows, looking straight at her. She was stunned. She knew he was an arrogant snob, but to doubt her work? and on what grounds? That she was young and new? Oh how she hated him! She stood up. She was not going to sit here and be ridiculed by this man, just because he was taking her pride in her work and smearing it in her face and seeming to get some kind of pleasure out of doing it.

"So that is how you congratulate an employee for their hard work Mr. Flair! Well, let me tell you something. You can fire me if you like. I can easily get another job elsewhere. I've worked hard here to prove myself, but if you don't like it or you find my work unsatisfactory then release me from my contract."

"On the contrary Shar; I find your work excellent. It excels my highest hopes for a new employee. As far as that goes, for my old employees also."

Shar stopped. She had just reached the door. She turned and to her surprise collided with Mark. She hadn't heard him coming up behind her. She dropped her purse when they collided but didn't bother to pick it up as Mark had caught her by the shoulders to steady her and her blood had already started to feel like fire was running through her veins from where his hands rested. She looked up into his eyes and their eyes locked.

A magnetic force beyond her control kept her from looking away. He was leaning closer; she knew he was going to kiss her; but even though her mind told her to run, her body wouldn't move. She had anticipated this moment ever since she first flew into Denver beside him on that plane, and she couldn't stop it now.

At first it was light and sweet, but then he was like a tiger freed from his cage. The passion rose and his kisses became demanding. She realized he would rape her right where she stood if something wasn't done fast to stop the man. She realized she had unleashed him and it was up to her to tie him back up. She thought about what she had said about the willing models who got what they deserved. She said "Come on Mark. Enough is enough!" She had turned her passion to ice, as fast as she had gone under his spell, pushing against his chest with her arms.

He realized how close he had come to blowing his whole plan. A few minutes of pain would hurt a girl like her but a heartache would last her a lifetime. He had to make amends for his actions and fast. If she left like this she would never come back.

"I'm sorry Miss McCoy. I don't know what possessed me to act like that. At first I just wanted to let you know I really do like your work; so that you wouldn't quit. I guess having a beautiful girl in my arms responding to me was more than I bargained for."

Shar was boiling mad now. To think that he had only kissed her to apologize for his rudeness; and then to insinuate that she had thrown herself at him; Well, he could go square to hell and back as far as she was concerned. The conceit of that man; when would it ever stop? She stormed out and slammed the door almost in his face. She went down to her office and her face was still red from anger as she entered. Carol looked up and said "Did you get a raise?"

"No. I'll be lucky if I don't get fired after what just happened." She said. Carol looked surprised. Shar shut the door. She told Carol of his accusations and how she had decided to stand up for herself. How he had stopped her as she was leaving. Carol was laughing when she said enough is enough. She left out the fact that she didn't want to stop because she had stopped him and that was what was relevant. Carol was laughing so hard and Shar thought that she was laughing at her. She said "It isn't that funny. I might lose my job over this and why? Because I'm young and good looking? Men! I hate them all!" Now Carol was laughing so hard she was crying.

"I wish I could have been there my little Shar; and to think I was worried about you losing your heart to him. I guess I can quit worrying now. It seems you got to him more than he got to you."

Shar didn't understand. All she knew was she had earned a raise and then blew it with her own temper. Now she was as mad at herself as she had been at him. Maybe if she had just listened. It was probably just his normal procedure and how she had blown it by taking everything so personal. Why couldn't she be objective when it came to what he thought of her? Was it that she wanted to prove to him so much that she was a lady not a child? But why should she care?

Shar was glad that the day had ended. All afternoon all she had done was start one design after another and they had all ended up in the wastebasket. That night she decided to call Tom. She had to know some man thought her a woman; instead of a child still wet behind the ears.

She was sure glad she had not bumped into Ralph again. What if the first time she saw Mark again she would have been trying to explain that? Maybe luck had fallen her way after all; she realized that Mark would have really thought her dumb then. Being the chauvinistic male that he was, he probably would have taken Ralphs word over hers no matter who was telling the truth. Well, at least now she would have a reputation to back her if it ever did occur. Chances were getting slimmer all the time that Ralph would recognize her. Especially since Mark hadn't and it had only been two months since they had sat side by side on a plane and Ralph photographed several models every day. Shar began to relax. Just four weeks until Tom would be back. Even if it would only be for a week or so it would be fun to see him again. She would invite him to the company party. Carol had told her they were giving a company Thanksgiving Ball for all company employees and they could bring a guest. Yes, that would give her a good excuse to call Tom without being too obvious. She didn't want him to get the wrong idea.

She sat on the bed pushing the buttons. What if he had found someone else? Well, that wouldn't matter. Tom was her best friend. She had only known him that one week, but she felt like she had known him all of her life. With Tom at her side she might be able to face Mark again and it was for sure he would be at the party. After all it was a party he put on for his employees. She was about to hang up when a lady's voice came on the other end. "Hinley residence; May I help you?"

"Is Tom in?" Shar asked.

"Which Tom; the third or the fourth?"

Shar thought that this must be his dad's house. "The fourth." she answered. "Just one moment; May I ask who is calling?" asked the woman.

"Shar McCoy." she replied. Then there was a pause; she must have put her on hold. It seemed like forever before someone picked up the phone. "Hello Shar, is something wrong?" Tom asked. He sounded excited. "No Tom, I just wanted to hear your voice of confidence, that's all."

"Wow, baby, you scared me. I thought something was wrong; now I find that it is better than alright. Did distance make your heart grow fonder?"

Shar laughed. "No. Don't be silly Tom. You know you are the best friend a girl ever had."

"A guy can hope can't he? After all where would we be without dreams?"

Shar laughed again. He had the best sense of humor and knew how to lift a girl out of the dumps. Then she remembered why she had called. "Tom?"

"Yes babe?"

"I was wondering if you would want to go to a company party with me when you are up here in November?"

"Hey; sounds good. Here I was wondering how I was going to get you away from the local chaps to have you to myself for an evening while I was there, and now you have solved that for me."

"Well now you can stop worrying." Shar said. "I'm doing really well at work, and I love Megan and Beth. They are both really sweet."

"I knew you would like them." Tom replied. He wasn't sure what to say to her about John so he decided to ask her. "Have you had any second thoughts about your previous engagement?"

"No." Shar said. "Why do you ask?"

"Oh I was just wondering. You know sometimes girls make rash decisions and then change their minds."

"Not me!" Shar said. "John is definitely a thing of the past. In fact I haven't even thought about him since I told you about him that night. I was definitely lucky to have broken up with him before we tied the knot. Looking back now I don't even know what I saw in him."

Tom had to wonder if she would feel the same about him someday. The John he had met was not the kind of guy a girl just dumped and forgot. No wonder Shar just thought of him as a friend after having a guy like John wrapped around her little finger. She was going to be one hard dish to scoop; but she was well worth the effort. "Well, you can count on me Shar. What day is the party so I can plan my trip around it?"

"It's the 22nd of November. Thanks Tom. You won't be sorry; I promise I'll look my best."

"Is that any better than the night we went out?"

"Of course; I'm older now and more sophisticated." Shar laughed. It was fun to tease Tom.

"Not too much, I hope. I'd hate to think I stopped that last night just to save you for someone else." he said. Then he laughed and Shar knew he was just teasing her again.

"Until November when you get here;" She made a kissing sound almost like a cow pulling its foot out of a mud hole, laughed and hung up the phone.

Lying back on the bed she hugged the pillows he had bought for her and wondered why she even cared what Mark thought about her. Tom was ten times the man Mark was. He was sweet, forgiving, friendly, passionate, very good looking, a perfect escort, so why couldn't she feel when she was with him the way she felt when she was in Mark's arms? It just wasn't fair that Mark could make her so emotional when he was such a butt of an egotistical man; stuck only on himself; to the point of walking on all of the women around who were stupid enough to fall for him. Try as they would to please him, he was like a cougar who liked nothing better than the hunt. Once he had attacked and killed his prey on to the next hunt. Well, she was going to make sure that the hunt never ended in her case. She knew that she could not stand to be just another of his conquests. He was so arrogant she thought he probably keeps a record in a little black book of all of his trophy's. Shar laughed at herself. Here she was thinking of Mark not five minutes after she had called Tom. In order to get Mark off of her mind she walked into the living room where Megan was writing home and Beth was watching T.V. "Want some dinner? I'll cook." she said. Megan had already eaten on her way home and Beth said a soup and sandwich would be fine, so Shar walked into the kitchen.

CHAPTER 9

Mark could not believe it. He was spending thousands of dollars to find Shar McCoy and she had been right here the whole time drawing a paycheck from him; while she spied on his company. This was quite a scheme young Tom had come up with. Of course the last place he would look would be in his own employees. He went back over all of the designs Shar had turned in. They had all been terrific sellers. It was quite a record. In two months three of her designs had been #1 sellers. Tom must be paying someone a pretty penny to design for her. Too bad Tom doesn't realize how good they are and start using them himself. He would have to check to see if any of them were copies of the Hinley Companies in Houston. Why did she have to be so gorgeous? Why did they have to meet under these circumstances? Maybe she was as innocent as she looked. Maybe she needed the money and Tom had taken advantage of her in her time of need? He would not like to punish her if she was innocent. Then he would be just as bad as Tom was for using her need to make her go against her own principles. He would check her records and find out if her parents were sick and poor, then he would decide what to do next. How he hoped that it was Tom's doing.

He called his secretary. "Contact the Mellor Detective Agency and have the call put through to me." he said. It wasn't long until Mr. Mellor was on the phone. "I was surprised to hear from you." he said. "I was about to call you and suggest that we give up this search. There hasn't been a trace of Shar McCoy in Houston unless she has a different identity."

"No I have found her myself." Mark replied. "I would like one of your men to go to Yakima Washington and find out if her parents are poor or are having any kind of hardships."

"It's your money." Mr. Mellor replied, "But this I will throw in for expenses only since you found her yourself, and my detectives couldn't. By the way; where did you find her?"

"Right here in Denver." Mark replied.

"Well I'll be. We'll talk to you in a couple of days and thanks for your patronage." Mr. Mellor replied.

Mark sat the phone down. He couldn't think of a way to get Shar to talk to him again, but he would come up with something. He had made lots of women mad before, but they were always eager to make up.

When Shar awoke that morning she felt like sleeping all day. She hit the snooze button and it seemed like only seconds before it buzzed again. She knew that she had to get up now or she wouldn't have time to shower and get ready for work on time. She climbed out of bed and went to shower. It was drizzling rain she noticed as she passed the window. It looked as though winter was setting in. She knew she was going to have to go shopping for a winter wardrobe soon. Maybe the coming weekend they could make a day of it if Beth or Megan wanted to go; maybe even both would want to go. That would be fun.

She dried off briskly in front of a heater in the bathroom because she hadn't turned the thermostat up in her room and it was very cool. She preferred to sleep with the heat down and the window open a little when it didn't rain. She slipped into her robe and walked to her closet. She decided to wear a black pantsuit with a silver blouse that was one of her warmer outfits. She could remove the jacket if she got too warm at work. She put it on and smiled at her reflection in the mirror. The outfit fit her to the tee. She hadn't gained any weight but some had transformed itself from her thighs to her bust. Now the jacket was filled out and the pants fit perfectly. She thought back to all of the tennis she had been playing and decided that it must be doing her good in more ways than one.

She put the finishing touches to her long dark lashes and stood up satisfied that if Mark called her to his office today he would look twice before condemning her. It gave her a feeling of confidence that just yesterday he had so easily taken away from her. She felt good and knew that today would prove to be a productive day.

She was the first to go into her office and to her surprise there sat a dozen long stemmed roses; beautiful red roses on her desk with a card on them. Tom she thought. How sweet of him to remember the roses. She opened the card and read "Sorry about yesterday, will see you for lunch Mark."

How could he assume that she would jump at the chance to eat with him after the way he had treated her the day before? And, how could he know that she didn't already have plans made to eat with someone else? She would make it plain for him to see. She would return the roses with a note saying, "You're forgiven but I already have a lunch date with someone else. Sorry. Shar."

She called to one of the runners who took designs to different departments and asked him to deliver the roses to Mr. Flair's office. "Have his secretary put them on his desk." Shar smiled to herself as she started to sketch. This dress could be called the temptress she decided for that was the mood she was in. The neck would come down off of the shoulders and the cups in the front would have the shape of a heart; it would have a slim fitting waist with a bell shaped skirt; the sleeves would be like two butterfly wings just touching at the top with a stitch. There it was done; what a look. It had a look all its own; revealing yet concealing. She wondered if she should keep it and have one made for herself for the Thanksgiving party. No; she decided; she did it on company time so she would turn it in and have to come up with another for herself on her own time, or just go buy one. She was shading it in from a salmon color on the top down to a very vivid pink at the waist and back almost a shade past salmon at the bottom. Then she made a note to also go the opposite direction with the colors starting at the top with the vivid pink shading to salmon color and back again. The back was an oval opening down to the waist. Now that it was done she started to work on a house dress; simple, feminine and comfortable. It would be very small checkerboard print using pastels with white puffy sleeves to elbow length. It would have pleats from the waist up in the back to make room for comfortable shoulder movement. It would have a V neck with a fold down collar and a round circle skirt. It would button in front down to the waist and have a matching belt.

Shar was pleased with herself. Two dresses out and it wasn't even lunch time yet. Carol said, "What's gotten into you today?" when Shar handed her the designs to check over. "These are great! Trying to get another appointment with the Lion?" She laughed. "This checkered one will be a best seller you can bet on that at the locals and this other one could be sold as a McCoy original." Then she laughed handing them back to Shar. She stopped laughing as the door was swung open and Mr. Flair stormed in. He closed the door then he looked at Carol. "Can you go take a break or find something else to do for five minutes? This won't take long!" He smiled at her warmly.

Reaching out Shar accepted the designs from Carol, as Carol almost tripped over her own feet getting out of there. Mark opened the door for her and pulled it shut behind her; saying thanks to her back as she exited.

When he turned back to Shar she could see by the look on his face that she was in for a good one. "Why may I ask;" his voice was as calm as the air before a lightning storm; "did you have the roses I sent you for a job well done, put back on my desk? I expect my employees to accept the bonuses I give them with gratitude. Not to have them throw them back in my face. Also when I want a confrontation with an employee over lunch, I expect them to put business over pleasure and cancel any previous arrangements. Do I make myself clear, Miss McCoy?"

"Yes sir, but I was under the impression that we were not paid for our lunch hours; therefore, this company has no control over what we do during that time."

Mark was losing his control. He could not make a scene here. There were too many eyes on him through the windows. "Very well Miss McCoy. You do whatever suits you on your time but, at 1 o'clock sharp you report to my office and you go out to lunch with me while I eat and try to have a civil conversation with you. Do you understand? Don't be late!" He walked out and shut the door.

As soon as he was gone Carol came busting through the door. "What did he want? Surely he didn't fire you over yesterday did he? Boy. I've never seen Mr. Flair so worked up over anything."

Shar had to tell Carol of the roses and the invitation that was on her desk when she came in that morning.

"And you sent them back? Are you crazy? Long stemmed red roses! Do you have any idea what those cost this time of the year? ...And to turn down his invitation to lunch; that must have been a first for him! Every girl I know would give their eye teeth to go to lunch with him." said Carol.

"It wasn't that I couldn't forgive him for yesterday." said Shar. "It's just the way he went about it. Asking or rather telling me it was ok just because he can afford flowers and to think that because of his money he can tell people who they can eat lunch with. Well, I wouldn't break my lunch date to please him so he told me to report to his office at 1 o'clock sharp and go out to lunch again with him. That was an order!"

Carol was laughing. "Boy has he got it bad for you? Normally he would have just fired anyone who stood up to him like that, or put him off. He is not a very patient man. He is used to getting his own way. His father started this company when Mark was very small and it has always been a successful business, however, Mark is a much better business man than his father was."

Shar was trying to think of a good place to go for lunch where no one could see that she didn't really have a date. She couldn't go downtown. If the traffic got bad she would never make it back in time for lunch with Mark. She couldn't eat nearby and she couldn't stay there that was for sure. So she drove home grabbed a quick salad and ate it and drove back. That should hold her over while she watched Mark eat.

It was five minutes till one when she entered the lobby. She shook the rain off of her umbrella and went into the ladies' room to freshen up. She combed her hair and freshened her lipstick and eyeliner. She had better go up before Mark started looking for her. She didn't want to cause a scene again today; once a day was enough. She decided that no matter what he said to her she would be polite and nice back to him. No more tantrums.

Mark picked up his jacket to go when his secretary buzzed him; "Mellor Detective Agency on the phone." Mark motioned Shar out to the outer office, "I will be right with you." he said; "won't take a minute." He winked at her then shut the door. He strolled over to the phone. What bad timing he thought. "Yes. This is Mark. Did you find out anything?"

"Yes we did. Her folks are very well to do. You could say they are moderately wealthy compared to yourself. They are both healthy and Shar appears to be an only child. It seems as though her parents spoiled her rotten and so did all of the ranch hands. She has had everything her way since day one."

"Thanks." Mark said. "Send me your bill. Talk to you later Mellor; I have an appointment so I have to rush."

"Well Mark you can tell she isn't after you for your money. It has to be your charm or good looks." He laughed and hung up.

If he only knew Mark thought. She isn't after me at all; it's my company she is after, as if her and Tom's own fortunes couldn't keep the two of them for 10 or 12 generations if neither one of them ever worked a day.

This information put a new light on the picture. Now, how could he captivate her heart without ever letting her know just how much he despised her? Well, inwardly anyway. She could definitely turn a man's head with those looks and that figure. Then there were those eyes and that smile. He realized how much he wanted her physically, but he couldn't let that ruin the plan he had for her. Then she was so far in that there was no possible escape he would have her and close the trap. She would never forget him the same way he would never forget her. His dream model for the best campaign ever to have to be put on ice. All because of two overly greedy rich kids who get a kick out of stealing, lying, and cheating others just to satisfy their own sick egos.

Shar was waiting patiently as Mark entered the outer office. He spoke to his secretary, then he and Shar left. He was a perfect gentleman throughout lunch. Shar said she had already eaten and ordered some hot tea to drink while Mark ate. He had a large steak, baked potato and salad with apple pie ala-mode for desert. Shar sat content to watch him eat. He was so masculine she could easily find herself daydreaming about him if she didn't watch herself. "What exactly did you have to talk to me about that couldn't wait?" she asked.

He smiled. He would play to her greedy side he decided. "We can all use more money can't we?"

"Sure." she replied.

"Well I'm offering you a raise. It is subject to your designs. The better they sell the more money you make. You are the first employee I have done this with, so I would like to keep this agreement between the two of us. I don't want any hard feelings. I am kind of experimenting with this idea on you to see if it helps to keep production at its very best. You seem to be on a roll, so it should be quite a little bonus for you on your better weeks. It's only going to be 2% of sales profit but the longer each dress stays on the market the bigger and better your royalties will be. I will take you to lunch each Friday and you will get a report on how business is going and your bonus check directly from me. No one else is to know about this. From now on you will meet with me on your lunch hour on Fridays and lunch will be on me. If you want other dates, set them on your other days please."

She smiled. He could be quite polite when he wanted to. Maybe she had judged him too harshly at first. Mark was a perfect gentleman and by the time it was time to go back Shar was enjoying herself immensely. She was looking forward to the next Friday and she decided she would prove to him that his new plan would work; even if she had to spend her evenings thinking up new ideas. The next three weeks went like clockwork. As smooth as smooth could be and each Friday Mark faithfully called her at 8 o'clock to confirm their lunch date. Rumors were flying around the office and Carol couldn't be told the truth as to why she spent each Friday dining with the boss.

One morning the phone rang and Carol answered it. "This is Mark is Shar there" he asked.

"Sure, isn't she always? Except for 1 till 2 on Fridays; those are her afternoons to success." Carol handed the phone to Shar. She took it giving Carol a dirty look.

"What was that all about?" Mark asked.

"Oh nothing, it's just one of those days. You know." Shar wasn't sure what was eating at Carol, but there had to be more than just what met the eye. She had to stick up for Carol because Carol was her friend.

"See you at one then?" he asked.

"Sure. See you then." Shar put the phone down and went over to Carol.

"What's up Carol? I know something or someone is getting to you; now out with it."

"Oh it's nothing Shar; just rumors. You know the way they talk about the boss and whoever he is sleeping with this week. Well, you are usually out with Mark on Fridays so that's when the cantina really buzzes. Like

I wonder how early they will leave the Thanksgiving party. Surely they couldn't stay at a public party together all evening and him keep his hands off of her. Now they have started a bet as to what time Cinderella leaves the ball with Prince Charming, as they call him."

Shar laughed; "Well, don't put a bet in because Cinderella isn't coming to the ball with Prince Charming as they call him, but with a real prince all her own. That should make their eyes boggle and their tongues wag."

"Shar do you mean you aren't getting stuck on Mark?"

"No I'm not. Fridays are strictly business and you can meet Tom at the party."

Carol smiled and hugged her. "Now I can't wait for the 22nd to get here; just to see their faces. I'm not going to say a word beforehand. Anyone who is dumb enough to make bets on gossip deserves to lose their money."

Shar's day went by fast. She had been putting every ounce she had into this experiment so that Mark would get a real taste of how the real designer would react. Also the more she got to know Mark the more she had to win his heart. Sometimes she would catch him with his guard down and she would see a gleam of pride there. He must like her more now. They seemed to grow closer every time they met. She was glad that she had invited Tom to the party though.

That would put a damper on the fast tongues and she didn't want her Fridays to stop. She lived each week for that one hour but Mark couldn't know that until she was sure he loved her as much as she loved him.

Carol said, "Aren't you going to lunch? It's 11:45 you had better get ready for the big day." Carol was smiling brightly at her; anticipating her day at the ball. Shar wondered if Carol would be smiling if she knew the truth. That Tom was just a deterrent, because she would be unable to keep her guard up all evening in Mark's arms.

CHAPTER 10

They were through with lunch and Mark asked her to dance. He was a perfect dancer; holding her just right not to close and not to lose. They moved around the dance floor as one. Shar loved this. She closed her eyes and wished that it would last forever. Then Mark's lips lingered on her forehead. Desire started to pulse through her body increasing by the second. She wanted to pull his head down and plant one on him but she knew if she did that it would be the end of her dream. She looked up and he looked down to see the ice blue fire blazing with desire. They melted his very soul and he wanted nothing more than to have and hold her forever. "Shar come to the ball with me please."

She stopped. She couldn't believe he had asked her. She had asked Tom because she was sure he would be with another girl. Now she had to turn him down over her own stupid stunts; but then again, it would serve its purpose, to shut up the rumors at work. She also knew that Mark might like her but it was far from the love she felt for him and she couldn't let him know of his power over her to soon. "Mark, I can't." she replied.

"Can't or won't?" he stepped back looking down at her angrily.

"I've already asked someone else." she answered truthfully.

Mark looked upset and Shar couldn't understand why; probably because he hadn't gotten his own way. He had a way of doing that, so Shar let it pass. She got her wrap and waited by the door. He paid the tab, left a generous tip and they left.

"Don't think I'll go by myself and you can bet I will be there. It's my party you know."

Shar smiled hiding her pain within. She wanted to reach out and caress the line of his jaw and tell him that she loved him and that this was all setup a month ago; but she couldn't take that chance. It wasn't his heart that ached as hers did. It was only his ego.

Shar found the perfect dress in a formal shop. It was made of light blue rayon that clung to every curve of her body. The neck was low and it had no straps. There was a see through net wrap that was the same color of blue with rose buds woven on it. She had her hair done at a local beauty shop; braided into a crown around her head with nineteen light blue roses braided in among the strands of honey gold hair. She looked better than she ever had before. As she looked in the mirror she realized how Mark's eyes would shine when he saw how really pretty she was. He had never seen her dressed up. The light blue heels matched the dress perfectly. She finished her make up with a little light blue eye frost and was ready and waiting when the doorbell rang.

Shar hurried to open the door for it had been three months since she had seen Tom and right now she needed a friend. She flung open the door for a big hug and there stood Mark in a tuxedo. "I just had to stop and see you first before going to the party," he said. "I brought you a gift." and he held out a small package. "Shar you are more beautiful than your picture."

"My picture?" Shar looked stunned.

"Than what I pictured." he commented covering his mistake.

"Well, thank you Mark. I take that as a compliment."

"You should and it was." he said.

Shar had opened the package and in it was the most beautiful teardrop necklace; a diamond tear dropping from a gold chain with two floating gold hearts, one on each side of the diamond.

"Wear that tonight for me please. I had it made far you Friday after you turned me down for someone else. Well, I have to go pick up my date. Hope to see you there." He fastened the chain around her neck and kissed her lightly on the side of her neck pulling her to him. She could feel his taught body wanting her, but she couldn't say yes. Not here. Not now. Tom would be here any second and Megan was in her room. "See you there." she said managing to sound calm and collected.

She considered the situation leaning against the door; her eyes closed; after Mark had gone. All of her life, when she had wanted something she had gone after it with every ounce of her being. Her desires knew no bounds. Painful reality struck her. She wanted Mark and her desires were winning against her conscience, memories, fear, and reason. How could she keep going on with her heart and body fighting her mind and her heart being ripped apart in the middle of it all. Mark didn't know how true the necklace she wore was for tonight. He got it as a joke to help heal his ego; knowing that even with another man she wore his chain. How real the joke was she thought.

There was a knock at the door. Shar opened it half expecting Mark to be standing there. Instead there was a low wolf whistle and there stood Tom; arms out stretched and Shar almost jumped into them she was so happy to see him. He was in a white tux and with his dark curly hair Shar had to admit he was the handsomest man she had ever laid her eyes on.

"Turn around and let me look at you babe. You know when you said you would out do yourself tonight I thought that it was impossible, but darling you have definitely done it. I only wish I was taking you back to Houston to show my dad instead of to a company party where you will be showing me. I know how these things go. I've been to them before, so I tried to look my very best for you too" said Tom.

Shar laughed then. He had a way with her that made her forget all of the other things in life except for the moment at hand. Why couldn't she be more like him and live just for the moment instead of always getting tangled in her own webs.

"Are you ready for the grand march?" he asked as they pulled up in front of the disco that had been reserved for the party.

Shar said, "With you Tom. Lead the way." As they entered the building all eyes turned towards them and Shar was glad for Tom's support. He started to hum here comes the bride in her ear and she started to laugh. If only they knew what he was saying to her. Then she thought of Mark. Was he here yet? Was he one of those faces?

She hadn't seen him yet. Carol came up grinning from ear to ear. "You should have heard the whispers about Mark already tiring of you, when he came in with her," Carol told her the first chance she got. That was when Tom had gone to get some punch. "Bet you could have heard a pin drop when you showed up with your knight in shining armor. Where did you find him? He even makes Mark look almost human."

Shar laughed at that. She had thought Mark had looked human ever since that first day on the airplane. A very powerful one, but definitely Masculine Humanity.

Mark was wondering who this man was that Shar had brought to his party, but from that distance he could not make him out. Just listen and hope someone would know who he was he decided.

Tom came back and asked Carol to excuse them. "You understand; we've been apart for three months. I would like to hold Shar for a while. Care to dance?" he said turning to Shar.

"I'd love to." was her reply.

Mark heard the rumor after it had crossed the entire room. By then it was Shar has had a secret love for many months and they want to dance and hold each other. Mark was fit to be tied. He realized he was jealous of this man holding Shar and therefore his plan had backfired. He had been the one falling for her. Even knowing all about her bad side; he loved her still. He went out onto the terrace to get away. They had been dancing all night. Why wouldn't someone cut in so he could go dance with Shar?

Suddenly he had an idea. What did he pay people for? He was looking for Matt. He knew Matt like the back of his hand. He would go get Shar for him with a little encouragement. He found Matt dancing with a model. "Matt." he said; "Why don't you go break up the little love nest and bring Shar over here to me, if you just waltz her over here she will never know your plan."

"Sure boss. It sounds like fun to me." Matt laughed, and away he went off into the crowd. Shortly he was back with Shar in his arms. "Care to cut in boss?" he said.

Mark said, "Sure." Taking Shar in his arms he waltzed her out across the floor, he bent his head inhaling the aroma. She was wearing Chanel 15 and how scrumptious she made it smell. He never wanted the song to end as they danced through the night.

Suddenly there was a hand on Shar's shoulder. She turned to see Tom; cold anger flashing in his eyes. "Shar." he said. "You could have told me the truth about why you wanted me to come!"

Shar didn't understand. Tom had turned and was walking toward the door. She couldn't let him go. Someone had hurt him and he was her friend.

Mark said, "Stay Shar. I'll take you home." but Shar couldn't follow her heart, she had to help Tom, after all he was only there to help her.

The tears were streaming down her face as she raced through the parking lot to Tom's car. He was just climbing in. "Wait Tom!" she said as she jumped in and slammed her door. "I must know what happened."

"What happened!? You must think I'm pretty dumb! But, of course; you didn't know that I had met John; your ex-fiancé."

"John, my ex-fiancé? Where may I ask did you meet him?" Shar was wondering what had brought all of this on.

"I met him in Houston. He came to accuse me of sleeping with you and demanded that I tell him where you were; but I thought that if you wanted him to know you would have told him yourself, so I just put him off. Apparently he found you or you changed your mind and found him."

"I haven't found John; or him me as far as I know, so why don't you just tell me what upset you in there?" said Shar.

"When I walked up to cut in and saw how you and John were holding each other I knew you still loved him and that I didn't have a chance." Tom said.

"Wait a minute. Why do you keep calling my boss; Mark Flair; John? Where did you ever get that idea?"

Tom told her all about the man in there named Mark Flair; who apparently for reasons unknown came to Houston to find out if we actually were having an affair at the Hilton.

"Oh my God!" Shar said, covering her face with her hands. She realized the truth was being forced agonizingly to the surface. She really hadn't been free and on her own at all. Her dad had paid Mark to accept her as an apprentice in designing and also to make her feel successful at it. The whole time he had been playing with her to keep her from being on her own in the outside world. She had to prove herself. She looked at Tom. "I don't love you," she said, "but you are my best friend. Would your company hire me to work for you if I came back to Houston?"

The light was back in his eyes, "My sweet princess! Of course we will. I thought you had deceived me and all the while it was you being deceived." He reached out and pulled her into his arms. "Shar I love you and I will always be here for you." Shar knew what she must do to be able to face the future and go on living with her shredded heart. She must first face Mark and then her parents. Tomorrow would be soon enough for that; right now she was content to let Tom hold and console her.

Mark couldn't stand it anymore. He didn't care that she loved another man he had to go out and make sure she was alright. Not walking home in the rain. He didn't see her until he had gotten into his car and swung it around to leave. Then his headlights shined directly into Tom's car. There they were as plain as day. Yes she had caught up with Tom and from the way they were snuggled up they could have each other. He headed for home.

After parking his car in the garage he walked down a stream path that he had walked many times during the past three years. What could he do he wondered. He couldn't stand to have conquered the world, only to have lost his heart again to someone he couldn't have. He really cared for her and wanted to share his empire with her. He realized that he wanted Shar to mother his children; to be his wife; to come home to her every night. Had he played around so long that he had to lose her? He now realized what she had become to him. A reason to live! A reason to be successful! He wanted a son with her courage and her temper and of course with those fiery blue eyes. It was turning daylight when he had decided what he had to do. He walked up to the house whistling and went in; shaved; showered and got ready for work.

Shar was awake at the crack of dawn planning her future. She would get everything packed so that she could leave for Houston as soon as she had talked to Mark. Maybe with time her heart would heal and she could forgive her parents. She slipped into her tight blue jeans and loose sweat shirt. The ones she had worn that first day when they met on the plane. It seemed like an appropriate outfit to say goodbye in. She hated every ounce of him and every hair on his head for playing with her heart like it was a trinket. He was even more ruthless and cold hearted than everyone said he was.

She sat outside Mark's office door until he arrived. She thought; he's acting as though nothing at all has happened, as Mark unlocked his door. "Come in Shar. Are you working in those clothes? Today isn't a holiday you know." He turned to look at her as she entered, shutting the door for her.

"Who the hell are you working for?" Her voice shook with hysteria. She was losing control and she knew it but didn't care anymore. What did it matter anyway she didn't want him now? In fact, she despised him.

"Calm down Shar; I'll get you a drink."

"No!" She shouted. "I don't want anything from you or my parents! I figured it all out last night. You think I don't know that my dad paid you?"

Mark tried to interrupt; "Paid me for what may I ask?"

"You know very well what! You are the most despicable man I have ever set eyes on."

"And you are so sweet and innocent. Ha." Mark laughed. "The joke was on me. From the first time I laid eyes on you I knew you were trouble!"

"Yes. I bet it was hard for a man like you to keep your hands to yourself. My dad must not have known your reputation with women or he would never have done what he did. I know deep down he was just trying to protect me. I can't stand rich men! They are all too damned self-arrogant. They think they can buy happiness with their money. Well, it just doesn't work that way. I hope someday when you have a family you will let them go out in the world and find out for themselves. These jobs that are bought are not rewarding. I should have known that it wasn't my talent that was making me go places here; but no; I had to make a complete fool of myself and go out to lunch every Friday with the boss: I just bet you had a real laugh that day in your office when you called me in there and things got a little out of hand."

Mark was looking at her as if she had gone stark raving mad. He walked toward her, reached out and grabbed ahold of her arms. "Shar calm down, we must talk."

"Talk! Ha! I'm not through yet you weasel. Let go of me! I hate the sight of you." Tears welled up in her eyes. "Your touch repulses me, so let me go! You think you are a Don Juan or something that every woman just lives for the day when you look her way. Well, when you look at me it makes me sick to my stomach."

Mark had heard about all he could take from her. He strode back across the room from where he had walked to the window. He grabbed her and yanked her up to him. Shar saw the hate and anger in his eyes.

Maybe I've gone too far this time she thought. Now she was scared. He looked as though he could kill her as easy as to look at her. Then his mouth came down on hers punishing and bruising her gentle mouth. She fought trying to get away but his hand held the back of her head while his other arm encircled her shoulders. All she could do was struggle. His kiss was like no punishment she had ever endured. A part of her wanted to cling to him, while her mind screamed with the pain that he never loved her; never would; Oh God what did I ever do to deserve this, she thought.

His kisses were still hard but they changed from punishment to ecstasy. They were demanding a greater and greater response from her until she had no more fight left, and surrendered to them. She opened her clenched teeth and responded to the movement of his tongue. Her body arched against him and she could feel that his desire for her was as great if not greater than her desire for him. He kissed her eyes her nose her neck and then took possession of her mouth again. He had taken her far beyond the point of sanity and there was no way to say no now. Her desire had won and put her spirit in second place.

Mark had carried her to a couch where he continued to arouse every muscle in her body. She ached for him. Why wouldn't he just take her and get it over with? She wanted him so much, but he kept saying not yet Shar just enjoy. She was going to explode if he didn't give her more than just kisses and soon. She had never felt so helpless; so under his spell.

"Let's go to my house Shar. There is no privacy here."

"OK." she breathed. Anything to have him, she was so high in the world of ecstasy now that there was only one way down. She straightened her sweatshirt and Mark buttoned his shirt back up. "Can't start any rumors now can we?" he said. Shar walked down to his car in a daze. She got in thinking of how great it would be to give her virginity to Mark. He would be gentle and she knew he had more control than she did. He drove safe but fast to his home. It was beautiful, sitting there in the hills; a seclusion all its very own. Reality tried to break through her conscience. How could she throw away her virginity to this man who only wanted her as another conquest? With no love or marriage or any respect at all. After all, hadn't it all started out as punishment for her over-active mouth.

CHAPTER 11

S he should have gone straight to Houston with Tom instead of going back to tell Mark off. She should have known he wouldn't take it lying down. Then she laughed. He probably would take it lying down. Mark looked at her. Was she drunk? She hadn't been making any sense since she walked into his office this morning. Then to submit to his advances and respond as she had. He was sure that she must have drugged herself or she was still drunk from last night. He couldn't take advantage of her in that state of mind, but he would enjoy seeing her face when she awoke naked in his bed not knowing if she had or hadn't. He smiled to himself, they had arrived.

Shar got out and walked into the house. Mark showed her where the bedroom was. She looked around; it was very masculine just as its owner was. There was a dark mahogany wood king size bed with a bookcase headboard; two night stands; a large dresser and a chest of drawers that all matched. At the foot of the bed was a beautifully kept cedar chest that looked as if it might have come across on the Mayflower. The urge to look inside for hidden treasure hit Shar and she laughed out loud.

She suddenly became very shy and nervous yet not knowing how to get out of the situation gracefully. Mark was talking. She hadn't been listening but what she heard was "The bathroom is through the door there if you don't want to undress in front of me." He was smiling; daring her with his eyes. Shar was still mad enough and just stubborn enough to do it. She loved him and wanted desperately for him to love her in return, but needing her was the next best thing. She smiled and pulled her shoes off. Mark smiled, wondering just how far she would go before her shy naive ways would stop her.

Much to his surprise she wiggled out of her tight blue jeans. It wasn't fair for any girl to have a body like hers. She was past exotic. He felt his body responding to the sight of her bare legs, then off came the sweat shirt over her head. Wow! She even surpassed his wildest dreams, with her slender figure. Not an ounce of fat; perfect curves; her breast rising and falling beneath the sheer silk bra. This girl was very definitely getting a response from him. He told himself to relax; what she had on covers as much as a bikini, but his mind wouldn't listen. He could almost taste her delicate skin; his mouth began to water. Then much to his surprise, she unhooked her bra and out came the most perfect set of breasts he had ever seen. He could almost feel their warmth under his hands. Next she stepped out of her panties and walked towards him. He was so hot he couldn't even move. She was so gorgeous as she sat down on his knee, He wanted her for his lover, his woman, his wife, but it had to be in the opposite sequence for it to be right. He carried her to the bed sliding her out of his arms, he turned and walked into the next room. He called his office and asked his secretary to put a call through to the local church and have the minister call him as soon as possible. Then he hung up and went in, got undressed and climbed into bed.

Shar's emotions were so jumbled up. She loved him but she hurt so much that she felt like crying and laughing at the same time. Why doesn't he just go ahead and take what he wants and throw me out? She thought.

Mark walked out to the kitchen and came back with a bouquet of flowers. He smiled, "For the bride to be." he said; She wished he would quit teasing her. To him it was just a big game but to her he was just twisting the arrow that penetrated her heart.

The phone rang and Mark went to answer it. What a time for interruptions thought Shar. How long was she going to be in this agonizing state before relief came? Mark was talking. "Yes it is an emergency. Yes, it must be done immediately." Finally, he had convinced the person on the other end. To Shar he said, "Pick up your phone Shar."

She looked around at the phone on the bedside table. "Why?" she asked.

No one knew she was here. Why didn't Mark hang up? He went to his closet, pulled out a white shirt and slipped it around her shoulders. "There," he said. "We are ready now."

The voice came over the phone, "Do you, Mark Flair, take this woman to be your lawfully wedded wife?" Then she heard Mark say "I do!"

"Do you Shar McCoy take this man to be your lawfully wedded husband? To love, honor, and cherish as long as you both shall live?" Shar heard her own voice echo, "I do!"

Mark slipped a ring out of the trunk as he talked. He is playing this a little too far she thought. Then the voice was saying "Put the ring on her left hand." and Mark slipped the most beautiful wedding band she had ever seen onto her finger. The voice came over the phone again; "You may now kiss the bride, and don't forget to come in tomorrow."

Shar slammed the phone down. He was ridiculing marriage. That was sacrilegious. She would let him have her because she had gone too far now to turn back but come tomorrow she would be out of here forever. She thought to her self that she was probably lucky to have found out before marrying him for real that he was sick. That voice would get monotonous if that ritual went on each night.

Shar was drowning in the depths of love and desire that his skilled hands were demanding from her. She ached for him. "Oh please Mark, please." she begged of him. Then Mark's mouth came down on hers and he rolled on top of her. She cried out with pain and pleasure as the conception took place. Mark caressed her gently as he lay still beside her. "Why didn't you tell me you were a virgin Shar?"

Shar was crying, not from the physical pain as much as the mental pain. Mark didn't understand. He thought he had hurt her. "Shar, next time will be better."

"Next time?" Shar stammered. "What makes you think there will be a next time?"

He gently caressed the hair out of her face. "It's you and me babe. I've seen how you respond and I know I can't resist you Mrs. Flair."

"Mark will you knock off this Mrs. stuff."

"You prefer Shar?" his eyebrows shot up. "Regrets so soon?"

Shar stared at him. She couldn't believe that he was teasing her about being upset. He was so cold but his eyes and hands were so gentle. How could he look so inviting?

He was kissing the tears away that streamed down her face. She licked her lips trying to resist, but the desire leapt back into her veins full force. Why did she love him so much? She responded immediately to him, to his every caress. She shivered with torment she wanted him so badly again. Why did her body forsake her? This time he was slow and easy. He took her to heights unknown to her existence. When they finished she held him so close and the aroma of his cologne smelled so good, she wanted it to last forever. She knew for her it would have to last a lifetime. She knew she could never love this way again.

Morning came too soon. Mark's arms were around her to remind her that it had not been a dream. As she moved to get up he pulled her close to him, "Not yet Shar," he murmured kissing the back of her neck. He began to caress her body demanding a response from her. How wonderful it would be if he only loved her. Guilt and shame overwhelmed her and the tears slid down her cheeks.

She couldn't let him see this. She must never let him know how much she loved him. Hadn't he more than gotten even for her calling him a few names for selling out to her father. Hadn't he taken the only sacred thing she had to offer any man she might ever marry? Now she neither had love or her virginity to offer. He had taken them both away. She could not respond to him now. She jumped up and ran into the shower. She had to get a hold on herself.

She stayed in the shower for a very long time. No matter how long she washed she didn't feel clean. Finally, she knew that she had to come out and face reality. She deserved everything that she got. Isn't that what she had said about the models that had let Mark use them? She put a towel around her and walked out to get her clothes. To her surprise Mark was not in bed.

The smell of bacon was coming from the kitchen. She dressed and combed her hair, then she walked in the direction of the aroma. To her surprise Mark was buttering toast and setting the plate on the table between two plates of bacon and eggs. He poured two glasses of juice. "Care to join me?" he asked, pulling out a chair for Shar.

Shar realized it wouldn't help to anger him so she said "Sure."

He smiled at Shar and she thought; he really looks happy for the first time since I met him. Wouldn't it be great if they could have breakfast together like this every morning for the rest of their lives? Stop dreaming girl she told herself.

"Can we go to the office after breakfast?" Shar asked. "There are some things I need you to take care of for me."

"First things first." he said getting up and clearing his dishes. Shar picked up hers and started for the sink. Mark walked into the other room and slipped into his jacket. He looked as normal as ever. Shar wondered if she still looked the same.

She protested when Mark stopped in front of the church. She couldn't believe that he wanted to confess his sins so soon. "Come on Shar." he said opening her door and putting out his hand to help her. She stepped out of the car. The church reminded her of the little church back home and it was all she could do to keep from crying. Mark had put an arm around her waist and walked her into the pastor's quarters. "Are the papers ready?" he asked. "I'm Mark Flair and this is Shar McCoy."

The minister smiled at Mark. "There will be a $25 fee plus a $10 filing fee."

Mark said "Sure," and handed over a $100 bill. "Keep the change for the rush job. Where do we sign?"

"Right here." said the minister. "May, come here. The kids are here." In walked a plump woman who must have been his wife. She smiled, "Lovely morning isn't it?"

Mark signed on the line and said "Here: Shar, sign right here." Shar signed her name. Mark turned and kissed her warm and gentle, said thanks to the minister and his wife who were apparently signing the same paper and they left.

Shar wondered what kind of church you had to sign a paper in order to donate money for your sins, but the thought left her mind as quickly as it had entered it. They were at the office and she knew what lay ahead of her. She had to get Mark to release her from her contract so she could go to work for Tom. She had to pack and tell Beth and Megan she would be leaving. She had no other choice now that she knew that her dad had bought her success here with Mark, and ruined her only chance for happiness.

Shar looked at Mark. "Do you mind if I take today off and pack my things? Under the circumstances I don't think I should continue to live with Beth and Megan."

Mark looked at her. "Under the circumstances I sure as hell hope you're not going too. Of course you can have off as long as you like. I don't really care if you never design another dress as long as you live. It makes no difference to me. It won't make me love you any more."

Shar was really hurt. He could have let her down a little easier, he didn't have to throw her out and laugh in her face before the sheets were even cold. He was even worse than rumors had made him out to be. I suppose his little donation eased his conscience, if he even had one. The further from him she got and the faster she did it, the better off she would be.

She caught a cab to her apartment, packed everything in boxes, went to Greyhound and had it sent home. She went back to the house and left Beth and Megan a note. "Have to leave. Here is next month's rent, till you can fill my room. I'll be in contact. Your friend, Shar." She filled her car with gas and headed home. She could not bear to see Mark and have him laugh in her face, her dad had deceived her, but that was just protective love, Mark had never loved her. The tears streamed down her face as she drove until finally she had to pull off and rent a motel room to keep from wrecking and hurting someone else. She stayed in her room for a couple of days. Finally, hunger overtook her disillusionment. She fixed her hair and went to the restaurant to eat. The woman there was the one who had rented her the room. "We were beginning to wonder what you were living off of." she said.

Shar attempted a smile. "I just didn't feel like eating."

"Wish I had that problem." stated the overweight woman, patting her over stuffed middle.

"You are just too good of a cook, that's all." said Shar. The woman was smiling now. Shar ate and paid the tab, packed her car and headed for home.

She was really surprised when she pulled into the drive at home two days later, to see Mark running out of her folk's house. At first she thought she was dreaming, but as he approached the car she knew she wasn't. He grabbed the car door and all but yanked her out of the car into his arms.

"You're all right. You're all right." he said kissing her hair, eyes, and mouth. "You know you scared the life right out of me Mrs. Flair."

"I'm not your wife, so please don't make a fool out of me in front of my parents Mark."

"Yes you are. Those vows were real and you signed the marriage license at the church in front of the minister and his wife confirming it. And you can't say the ritual wasn't consummated, because I know I wasn't dreaming and you are either coming home with me or I will just have to become a wheat farmer because I love you and you are mine." Shar threw her arms around his neck. "Oh Mark! I love you too!"

Printed in the United States
By Bookmasters